Someone to SHADOW

Someone Series Book 5

ROBERT LEWIS

4 Horsemen
Publications, Inc.

Published By: 4 Horsemen Publications, Inc.

4 Horsemen Publications, Inc.
PO Box 417
Sylva, NC 28779
4horsemenpublications.com
info@4horsemenpublications.com

Cover & Typesetting by Autumn Skye
Edited by Kris Cotter

Library of Congress Control Number: 2024936481

Paperback ISBN-13: 979-8-8232-0397-5
Hardcover ISBN-13: 979-8-8232-0398-2
Audiobook ISBN-13: 979-8-8232-0495-8
Ebook ISBN-13: 979-8-8232-0396-8

Dedication

As always, I dedicate this book to my parents, Robert O. Lewis and Dolores C. Lewis. To my darling diva Bonita, who keeps me focused on writing. To my friends, whose love and support keep me going: Randy, Chris, Rodney, Berto, William, Jeff, Brian, and Kalvin. I also have to dedicate this to two of my favorite characters in this series: Jordan Hudson and Billy Turner.

These events occur at the same time
as those in *Someone to Marry*.

Table of Contents

BLOW JOBS

"**B**ILLY," JORDAN PROTESTED weakly while lifting his hips up to let his lover pull his shorts off. "You're shooting this week. We're not supposed to be fooling around."

Billy tossed the shorts to the side, then went to work liberating Jordan from his underwear. "Just because I'm shooting this week doesn't mean I can't make you shoot."

"You're going to get in trouble with Hunter," Jordan argued feebly, watching Billy settle between his legs.

Billy ran his hands up and down his boyfriend's legs. "You know oral is okay." Billy licked Jordan's length, sending shivers through him. "And I'm not leaving without the taste of you in my mouth."

"We're going to be late picking up Carlos." Jordan let out a gasp when Billy's mouth surrounded the head of his cock. Feeling the swirl of Billy's tongue, Jordan leaned back and ran a hand through his blond lover's hair. "I guess we can be a little late."

Pulling his mouth off Jordan's dick, Billy grinned up at him. "That's the spirit."

"Don't talk when your mouth should be full." Jordan pushed Billy back down onto his cock. Feeling Billy's warm mouth eagerly swallowing him down, Jordan moaned, "Fuck, Billy."

Jordan looked down to see Billy watching him. He saw the mischief in Billy's eyes as he suckled the tip of the cock. He watched Billy slowly swallow his cock. Billy let out a groan of satisfaction when his face was pressed into Jordan's groin. Billy began gliding his fingers over Jordan's legs.

"Holy fuck!" Jordan jolted in pleasure from the feel of Billy's tongue rolling like waves along his shaft. "Where did you learn that?"

Jordan watched Billy pull back to his tip. He moaned as Billy swaddled his cock head with his tongue. Billy's hands moved under Jordan's shirt and began to explore his soft furry belly. Jordan's breath hitched at Billy's soft, tingling touch. He loved that Billy made him feel sexy and wanted.

Fisting Billy's hair, Jordan fought the urge to thrust his hips up, choosing to let Billy set the pace. He leaned back and enjoyed the feel of Billy's soft lips wrapped tightly around his cock. He smiled at the sound of Billy's muffled moans. He knew he was the only one that got to hear him moan like that.

Billy made his money having sex, but that was just for show. With Jordan, he didn't have to worry about lighting, positioning, stopping and restarting while

maintaining an erection, or orgasming on command. With Jordan, he got to enjoy himself and focus on his partner.

"Billy," Jordan growled through clenched teeth, "I love what you're doing, but I'm not dealing with Paris if you two miss your plane."

Billy raised his head from Jordan's lap. He had a wicked glint in his eye. "You want me to get you off?"

"Billy…" Jordan warned, watching Billy make a small bottle of lube appear. "Don't." Billy slicked up two of his fingers on his right hand. "Control yourself."

Lifting Jordan's legs, Billy rested them on his shoulders. "I will." Billy pressed his fingers to Jordan's hole. "I promise." Billy slipped his fingers into Jordan, causing him to gasp. "Now, let's see if *you* can control *yourself.*"

"Oh, Billy." Jordan's voice went low and deep with lust from Billy wiggling around his insides. "Don't tease."

Billy kissed Jordan's cock. "Who do you love?"

"Not you if you don't get that mouth back on my cock!" Jordan pushed him back down on his throbbing cock. Billy worked his lover's length in time with his finger strokes. "Billy! Fuck!" Jordan flailed about in pleasure overload. "Please, Billy, make me cum before I rip your clothes off and ride you!"

Billy twisted his fingers and flicked his tongue over Jordan's cock head. Jordan's hole tightened. His legs stiffened, causing him to buck his cock up and down Billy's throat. His arms thrashed about wildly, knocking the pillows from the couch. Jordan's dick detonated in Billy's mouth.

"Holy! Oh … my … Billy!" Jordan blurted out as the orgasmic tremors shook his body.

Billy lowered Jordan's legs and pulled off his softening cock. He smiled with satisfaction as the last jolts hit his boyfriend and asked, "Who do you love?"

"You, you evil bitch," Jordan panted.

Billy moved up Jordan's heaving body to kiss him. "I love you, too."

"I messed up your hair." Jordan ran a hand through Billy's disheveled hair.

Laughing, Billy rubbed his nose against Jordan's. "It was worth it."

"I need to get dressed so we can go pick up Carlos." Jordan hugged Billy. "I'm going to miss you."

Resting his head on Jordan's chest, Billy sighed. "You'll be there Friday with Cameron."

"Are he and Carlos are still fighting?" Jordan ran a hand down Billy's back.

Exhaling loudly, Billy pulled away. "Yeah, all over that asshole, Alex."

"Hey." Jordan grabbed Billy's hand. "I don't know the specifics, but Cameron says it's strictly platonic."

Billy stood, pulling Jordan up with him. "Then why won't Cameron tell Carlos what it's about? Why all the secret conversations and text messages?"

"Do you remember how mad Carlos was when Cameron went to see Alex in the hospital?" Jordan pecked Billy on the lips.

Rolling his eyes, Billy snatched Jordan's underwear off the ground. "Yeah."

"We all have our issues with Alex." Jordan took his underwear from Billy. "But wasn't he your friend once upon a time?"

Billy handed Jordan his shorts. "That was before he changed. Cameron shouldn't be talking to him."

"You can't make that decision for him," Jordan said, slipping on his clothes. He cupped Billy's cheek. "Are you going to fix your hair or grab a hat?"

Billy huffed. "I'll fix my hair." He licked his lips. "I can still taste you."

"You're such a freak," Jordan laughed.

Billy winked at him. "You love it."

"That I do." Jordan patted Billy on his toned, taut ass as he passed by. Pulling out his phone, he checked his calendar. "Hey, Billy! Didn't you say Shadow and you filmed a scene that never made it to the site?"

From the bathroom, Billy shouted back, "Yeah, it was in the barn. Why?"

"No reason," Jordan lied. "Didn't he give you some advice when you told him you got a job offer?"

Billy stepped out of the bathroom, his hair slightly damp from fixing it. "Yeah, he told me to leave and don't look back." Billy studied Jordan. "Why are you asking about Shadow and me? Did you find a lead?"

"No." Jordan hated lying. "I'm thinking of pitching a story idea to Lexi about your relationship with Shadow. I just need some juicy tidbits to get her interested."

Billy snatched the keys off the hook and grabbed his suitcase. "You could pitch her the recipe for ice and she'd okay it. She trusts your instincts." Billy put an

arm around Jordan. "Come on, before Carlos starts blowing up our phones."

"Hey, Billy," Jordan leaned into him, "you know I wouldn't do anything to purposely hurt you, right?"

Billy cocked his head at Jordan. "Of course you wouldn't. Where is that coming from?"

"I, uh, I don't know." Jordan put an arm around Billy. "With Carlos and Cameron fighting, I felt like you needed to know that."

Stepping out the front door, Billy laughed. "When are the Chipmunk and Latin Lover not fighting?"

"When they're in bed," Jordan said with a laugh.

Locking the front door, Billy asked, "Are you going to be okay without me here?"

"Yeah. I've got work, and Drake and I are going to hit the gym together." Jordan squeezed Billy's biceps. "I got to get to your level."

Billy looked at Jordan with concern. "You know I love you no matter what, right? You don't have to slim down or change for me."

"That's why I love you." Jordan snatched the keys from Billy. "I'm driving. I'd like to get to the airport in one piece."

SHADOW IN THE WOODS

SHADOW WALKED UNEASILY along the front porch. For the millionth time, he was second-guessing his decision to do the video interview with Jordan Hudson. He had no guarantees that Jordan would honor their arrangement, especially since Jordan was dating Billy.

Jordan dating Billy was the only reason Shadow thought he could trust Jordan. Billy didn't love easily. Billy had been as skittish as a lost pup when he first got to the house because everyone he had loved had turned their backs on him. It was months before he let anyone truly in. That's when Shadow had really seen how beautiful Billy was.

Billy trusted Jordan enough to give him his heart. That was more than good enough for Shadow to trust Jordan with his story. Hopefully, doing the interview would finally put an end to all the speculations about him and ease the pain Billy obviously felt about not knowing what had happened to him.

Shadow stopped to pull a dead leaf from one of his potted plants. *Am I doing the right thing? What if someone figures out who I am? Where I am? Do I want to risk it?* he wondered.

He pushed the doubts away. He had to do this to give Billy closure and to give himself closure. He hoped that once the world, *once Billy*, heard his story, they would let him live in peace and obscurity. A footnote in the history of adult films that no one would ever read.

Shadow smiled upon seeing his husband leave his barn workshop with sawdust in his brown hair and his slight belly poking out of his varnish-stained overalls. He knew he'd have to remind Chris not to leave a trail of his work through the house. Then, while Chris was in the shower, he'd happily clean up said trail.

"Having second thoughts?" Chris kissed Shadow on the cheek, careful not to get his lover dirty.

Shadow's face brightened. "About the interview, no. About us? Yes, if you get sawdust all over my clean house."

"I'll strip in the mudroom." Chris took his hand. "Are you sure you want me there for this?"

Shadow noticed Chris struggling to get his fingers to intertwine with his. He smiled as he said, "Go take a shower, and I'll make you something to eat before the interview."

"I'm okay. I just pushed myself too hard trying to get the wood to talk to me," Chris argued.

Bringing Chris's hand to his lips, Shadow kissed it. "Humor me."

"Peanut butter and chocolate sauce sandwich?" Chris smiled coyly.

Shadow laughed. "Peanut butter and a little chocolate sauce sandwich."

"Are you sure you want me there?" Chris asked a bit more somberly.

Shadow nodded. "Yes, it's time you heard it all." His smile faltered. "Perhaps this way both Billy and I can have some closure."

"Are you going to tell them everything?" Chris shifted nervously.

Shadow closed his eyes and exhaled. "We'll see when it happens."

"I understand." Chris gave his hand a squeeze before letting go. "I'm going to go shower now."

Shadow watched his husband walk away and said, "Peanut butter and lots of chocolate sauce sandwich."

Chris turned and smiled at Shadow before going in the front door. Shadow thought to himself, *Why do I love that man so much?* He turned to look out into the surrounding woods. *Why did I love Billy so much? Is this going to help him or hurt him? Could this ruin his relationship with Jordan?*

Shadow went into the house. He picked up the broom he had left by the front door and began sweeping up the trail of sawdust, dirt, and woodchips Chris had left behind. He followed the trail to their downstairs bedroom, where Chris had left his clothes on the floor.

He picked up the discarded clothes and listened to his man singing "Rubber Ducky" off-key as he washed. *He's such a goofball.* After putting the clothes

in the hamper, Shadow took the dustpan he kept in the bedroom and swept up the rest of Chris's trail. He dumped the dustpan and looked at the bathroom door that was open a crack. *I guess we're both coming clean today.*

I'M ONLY DOING THIS FOR HIM

"**I HATED NOT TELLING** Billy, but I didn't want to get his hopes up," Jordan told Cameron over speakerphone as he fussed with his wild, uncontrollable hair in the bathroom mirror. "I really wish someone was here to help me get 'camera ready.'"

"Didn't Aunt Lexi send a crew over to help you?" Cameron asked.

Jordan looked at the phone guiltily. "I didn't tell her exactly what I was doing."

"What did you tell her?" Cameron asked suspiciously.

Jordan stopped trying to tame his hair. Timidly, he said, "I told her I was working on a project, but I didn't tell her what."

"Jordan," Cameron chastised.

Jordan began smoothing out the cream under his eyes. "You know she told me to stop hunting Shadow. And I did." He examined himself in the mirror. "He contacted me. He knew things that Billy told me, that only he and Shadow would know.”

“And if this turns out to be a bust like the others?” Cameron asked.

Jordan picked up tweezers and began plucking stray eyebrow hairs. “Then I didn’t get Billy’s hopes up and all I did was delay my flight to Hunter’s and Mark’s wedding.”

“Why is this so important to you?” Cameron continued his interrogation.

Jordan turned his head from side to side, examining his face. “Because it’s important to Billy, and Billy is important to me.” Satisfied he’d done his best, Jordan picked up the phone and left the bathroom. “My life changed the day Billy knocked on my door. I changed.” Jordan grabbed a water bottle from the refrigerator. “I owe it to Billy to do this.”

“You know Billy loves you no matter what,” Cameron commented. “You don’t owe him anything but your love.”

Jordan glanced at the time. His stomach twisted in knots. “It’s because I love Billy that I have to do this. If there is a slim chance that by doing this I can ease his pain and guilt. I’m going to do it. Consequences be damned.”

“What aren’t you telling me?” Cameron continued.

Jordan smiled to himself. “Watch and find out.”

“Got it,” Cameron said after a moment of silence. “Did you use me to interview yourself?”

Jordan turned the recorder off on his phone. “Got it on my side, too.” Jordan moved to the couch. “Hey,

you threw some of your own questions in there. Some good ones, too."

"Yeah, but I'm no Jordan Hudson." Cameron laughed.

Jordan leaned forward and turned on his laptop. "Alright, you quizzed me, now I get to quiz you." Jordan typed his password in. "Why are you with Alex instead of Carlos right now? What's going on?"

"He's going through some things," Cameron answered cryptically. "I'll explain more when you fly here."

Jordan looked at his phone, confused. "Fly there? Did you forget we're supposed to keep Billy and Carlos in line?"

"Paris can handle them, and I want you here for a day or so. We'll make it there for the wedding." Cameron paused. "There's a lot going on. I'll email you the details. I talked to Aunt Lexi about it, and she thinks it's a great idea."

Jordan thought for a moment. "Fine, but you can't tell Lexi what I'm doing."

"Okay, but you have to tell Billy and Carlos that we're arriving late," Cameron countered smugly.

Jordan groaned. "You and Carlos are still not talking?"

"Not without fighting." Cameron sucked his teeth. "I want to tell him what's going on, but after how he acted when I went to the hospital to see Alex, I knew he wouldn't understand."

Jordan winced at the memory. "Yeah, your Latin lover is passionate."

"He's stubborn, possessive, and drives me crazy," Cameron huffed. "He also makes me laugh and feel loved."

"How did we end up with two of the greatest oddballs?" Jordan noticed the time. "Cameron, I got to go. Email me."

"Good luck," Cameron said before the line went dead.

Jordan picked up the tablet beside his laptop. Opening his notes application, he sat it up off-camera so he could glance at his questions during the interview. Opening the video meeting program on his computer, he mentally debated changing locations. With time running out before the meeting, he decided he was in the best place.

He joined the meeting and waited, staring at his own image. He was a few minutes early. Those minutes felt like hours to Jordan as he waited. He felt the nervous knots cinching in his body. He wasn't sure if his nervousness was because this could actually be Shadow or about how he was going to tell Billy if it was.

The screen changed, relegating Jordan to the left side of the screen while a black box took up the right. A nervous voice came from the screen. "Hello, Mr. Hudson."

"Call me Jordan, please," he answered, trying to hide his own unease.

"You can call me Shadow." There was a long silence, making Jordan wonder if the mysterious man had ended the call. "I haven't been called that in a long time. It feels oddly appropriate."

"You know I have to verify your identity, as we discussed through email," Jordan reminded him.

Shadow let out a humorless laugh. "Yes, and as discussed, Billy isn't there, correct?"

"If you check his socials, you'll see that I dropped him and Carlos off at the airport earlier today. I made him post a picture." Jordan bit his lower lip and waited for Shadow to answer.

Shadow finally said, "He looks happy. I'm sure that's because of you."

"Thanks." Jordan relaxed a little. "Are you ready for me to record?"

There was some muffled talking before Shadow answered, "Yes. I hope you don't mind my husband is here. This will be the first time he hears some of this as well."

"Perfectly fine. Recording now." Jordan tapped a key. "Okay, what was the last video that you filmed with Billy for the Country Boyz site?"

Shadow let out a laugh. "Do you want the last video I filmed with Billy? Or the last one Billy believes he filmed with me for the Country Boyz site?"

"Excuse me?" Jordan asked.

"They're two different things," Shadow answered. "You see, I never filmed with Billy for the Country Boyz site. The last video Billy thinks he filmed with me was the two of us in the barn."

Jordan's face twisted in confusion. "What do you mean the last video Billy 'thinks he filmed with you?'"

"I'm going to tell you something that even Billy doesn't know…" Shadow paused. "I was in love with Billy. I was with Brett but fell in love with Billy. The

last scene he thinks he filmed with me was completely staged. I wanted to have one time that was only the two of us. That's why the video was never released. I kept the video for myself."

Jordan shifted uncomfortably. "You were in love with Billy?"

"Deeply. He loved me, too, but not the way I loved him. Billy only loved me as a friend," Shadow answered. "He loves you, though. I mean, he really loves you. You can see it in the pictures of you two together. The way he looks at you, even when you don't think he's looking. How he always touches you in some small way." Shadow laughed softly. "You're his future. I'm his past that could never happen."

Jordan smiled, remembering what he and Billy did before heading to the airport. "Billy is very touchy-feely. Of course, I'm not complaining."

"It's more than that, and you know it," Shadow accused. "I won't argue with you about it. You'll realize it, eventually. What's your next question?"

Jordan mulled over what to ask next. Finally, he asked, "What was the last thing you told Billy?"

"I told him to leave and never look back," Shadow answered quickly. "I wish I had taken my own advice sooner, if we're being honest."

A chill ran over Jordan. "You're… you're Shadow."

"That I am." Jordan heard the smile in his voice. "Now that you've verified my identity, what do you want to know?"

Jordan glanced at the questions on his tablet, then asked the first thing that came to mind. "Why did you reach out to me? Why did you agree to this interview?"

"I was asking myself those same questions right up to the moment I saw you on the screen." Jordan heard Shadow take a deep breath and let it out. "To answer the first question, I have to answer the second question."

Jordan leaned forward in interest. "Go on."

"I agreed to this interview because of Billy. I saw all the videos he made after what happened, asking for any information about me. I could see he was hurting because he didn't know what happened to me." Shadow's breath hitched. "It hurt me to know that by hiding, I was hurting Billy."

Jordan nodded. "I get that, but why did you reach out to me? You could have given your story to anyone."

"I wanted to give my story to someone I trusted. If Billy trusts you with his heart, I can trust you with my story." Shadow paused. "My husband and I have been following your career since the Country Boyz story. He's a huge fan of your short stories, and I really like how you have developed as a writer. I knew in my heart you were the right person."

Jordan felt a twinge of pride. "Thank you. I'm honored."

"I'm honored you agreed to do this," Shadow responded.

Jordan started to ask the first question on his list, then went with his gut. "How did you end up at Country Boyz?"

"The best place to start, the beginning," Shadow mused. "Without being too specific, you need some back story. I was a trust fund brat. When I say I was

a brat, I really mean it. I was young, arrogant, and wanted to do anything that pissed off my parents."

"I flunked out of college, and they sent me to our summer home in the middle of winter with the hopes that I'd straighten out my act." Shadow laughed. "Boy, were they wrong. Winter in the South isn't cold, but you can't go out on the water or sun yourself on the beach. That left two things to do. Drink and party.

"The only place to party was The Candy Shop." Shadow said the name with reverence. "That's where I met Brett. He was everything my parents hated. He was poor, had tattoos, and was cocky as fuck. Of course, I went home with him the first night. After we put on a show for everyone."

Jordan stared at the black square on the screen. "Tell me about that night."

POWER MOVE

*S*HADOW STEPPED INTO *the cinderblock building. The cheap lighting moved and flashed, trying to give the illusion they were moving with the music coming out of the blown-out speakers. It was still early and only about ten people were in the bar. A couple were on the dance floor, swaying to the beat. Four people were at the bar drinking and laughing. The rest were perched at various tables, scoping out the potential hook-ups for the night.*

He knew better than to risk a drink from the bar. The beer was room temperature. Their "top-shelf booze" was expensive bottles filled with the same cheap house liquor run through a water filter. The plastic cups and drink stirrers were often dug out of the trash, washed in dirty bar water, and reused.

Shadow sat down at a coveted table that everyone quietly acknowledged belonged to the local Gay A's. It was a social power move. If his parents were going to banish him to the swampy backwaters of the South, he was at least going to be part of its social elite.

After an hour, the bar started filling up. Shadow noticed the blatant looks and hushed whispers at him sitting at the sacred table. He didn't care. This was going to end one of two ways: he'd take his rightful place among the Gay elite or he'd be chased away. Either way, he'd get some sort of increase in his local stock value.

"You know this table is reserved?" a slender man in worn jeans and an athletic shirt said, sliding into the booth beside Shadow. He took a pull from his beer, then sat it on the table. "You'll have to find someplace else to lurk."

Shadow returned the man's cocky smile. "They don't reserve tables here."

"You must be new here." The man scooted closer to Shadow. "It's an unwritten rule that this table belongs to me and my business associate, Joe."

Shadow pitched his voice, so it sounded innocent and naïve. "Well, if it's an unwritten rule," his tone changed to defiant and arrogant, "then it's not a rule. You should have been here earlier."

"If I knew you were going to be here, I'd have shown up to hold the door open for you." The man leaned in to whisper into Shadow's ear. "Tell me your name, you cocky little fuck."

Shadow refused to be swayed by the man's seductive charms. "You sat down at my table. You first."

"I'm going to enjoy breaking you in." The man laughed arrogantly. "I'm Brett. Pleasure to meet you."

Shadow faltered. For some reason, he felt uneasy giving his real name. "Shadow. I wish I could say the same."

"Shadow." His fake name rolled off Brett's lips. "What are you drinking, Shadow?"

Shadow knew he had Brett hooked. He only had to keep him on the line. He turned his nose up. "Nothing this place serves. I have an aversion to hepatitis."

"We have that in common." Brett winked at him. "Come outside with me for a smoke?"

Shadow made a disgusted face. "I don't smoke."

"I don't either." Brett slipped out of the booth. He extended a hand out to Shadow. "Come on. Trust me."

Shadow took the offered hand and allowed himself to be pulled from the booth. Brett pulled him through the crowd of envious onlookers to the back door. Brett looked back and gave him a wink before pushing open the door and pulling them out onto the back patio.

Shadow saw the small band of smokers eye them as Brett pulled him off the back patio and toward the poorly illuminated parking area. He heard someone yell after them, "Get him, girl!"

"Here we are," Brett announced, after maneuvering them through the maze of cars.

Shadow pulled his hand back from Brett. He crossed his arms as he said, "You brought me out here to see your crappy car?"

"No." Brett pulled his keys from his pocket and popped open his trunk. He opened the cooler inside and pulled out two fresh, cold beers. He offered one to Shadow. "Fresh, cold beer without the risk of hepatitis."

Shadow took the beer and put it back in the cooler. "The last thing I need is beer on my breath when one of the country cops pulls me over and makes me suck him off to keep from going to jail."

"For someone new around here," Brett shut the trunk, "you sure know a lot."

Shadow moved closer to Brett. "I'm not new. That's why I know a lot. Like you're the big cock in town."

"The biggest." Brett smiled proudly. "Want to see?"

Shadow pulled Brett to him by his pants. He unfastened the top button and lowered the zipper. "I want to do more than see." He shoved his hand into Brett's underwear. He had heard that Brett was big, but he wasn't expecting the python that was quickly coming to life in his hand.

"Like what you feel?" Brett asked cockily. "It sure likes you."

Shadow made his voice as seductive as possible. "I'm sure it does. I'm sure you're going to like me, too." Shadow looked around. "What happens now? I suck you, maybe give you a little ass, you get off, and I become another conquest you forget about?"

"Yes, yes, yes, and no." Brett moved an arm around Shadow to cup his bubble butt. "You're definitely not one to forget."

Shadow pulled his hand from Brett's underwear. "Good." He shoved Brett's underwear and pants down. Brett's hard cock swung free in the night air. "You're big, but not the biggest I've ever had," Shadow lied.

"A professional." Brett moved so that he was leaning against the back of his car. "I've got an opening for a professional."

Shadow dropped down to his knees, grateful he was wearing shorts because of the uncommonly warm fall weather. He stroked Brett, feeling the man's dick getting harder and fuller in his hand. "If you're asking if I'm verse, I am."

"No, but that's good to know." Brett grinned wickedly. "Joe and I are opening a porn site. Using local country boys."

Brett put a hand on the back of Shadow's head. "You've got the look. Let's see if you've got the skills." Pulling Shadow onto his cock, he said, "Consider this an audition."

Shadow didn't hesitate to wrap his lips around the enormous cock head. He knew this was part of the initiation of getting into the exclusive local gay elite. You proved your value either through sex or money. He could have used his money, but that wasn't as fun as sex.

With one hand wrapped around the base of Brett's cock, Shadow worked down eight of the inches before he gagged. Pulling back to the tip, he was extra careful not to scrape his teeth along the delicate, hard flesh. He teased the tip with his tongue, then swallowed what he could of Brett again.

"That's it, boy," Brett moaned. "Swallow that fucking country dick. Give these nosey bitches a good show."

From the corner of his eye, Shadow saw the faceless crowd that had meandered over to watch them. A surge of excitement pulsed through him. With his free hand, he popped open his shorts and pulled out his achingly hard cock. Fisting his cock, he moaned a deep, lustful moan.

"That's it, baby," Brett encouraged. "Nurse off your new daddy's dick."

Another surge of excitement exploded in Shadow. He slurped Brett down, trying to get more of the jumbo dick into his mouth. Knowing there were strangers watching him during this casual, intimate moment was turning Shadow on, driving him to put on a show for them.

"You see this, bitches?!" Brett called out to the onlookers. "This is how you suck a fucking dick!" Shadow felt Brett's hands grip him on either side of his head. He knew what was coming next. "Take that dick, boy."

Brett started pumping his cock into Shadow's throat. Shadow gagged. He tried to cough between quick gasps of air, but he didn't fight it. He felt an odd sort of exhilaration at having his mouth used so openly in public. His hand was flying over his cock.

He could feel the excitement building in his balls. He raised up, feeling the tension in his body building. He was a rubber band about to pop. He was going to spill his load all over the ground, and he didn't give a damn who saw.

"God damn, you got a sweet fucking mouth," Brett grunted. "You better be ready to swallow or drown."

Shadow closed his eyes. He felt a strange calm consume him. He was breathing in time with Brett's thrusts. His throat relaxed, welcoming Brett in. The tingling readiness of his explosion held ready for the spark to ignite it.

"Swallow, boy." Brett stabbed his cock into Shadow's throat.

Shadow could feel Brett's dick throbbing in his mouth as it pulsed with each fire into the back of his throat. He swallowed, gulping as fast as he could as the sperm stream flooded his mouth. He could barely taste Brett's load before he had it down in his stomach and spilling out the sides of his mouth.

"That's my fucking boy." Brett smiled, watching Shadow nurse the last few drops from the tip. Addressing the crowd, he yelled, "You hear me, bitches?! This is my fucking boy!"

Leaning back on his knees, Shadow steadied himself with one hand while the other pumped furiously. The rubber band snapped. The spark ignited, and Shadow was thrusting his hips up into the air, jettisoning his creamy load up into the air before it splattered on the brown grass below.

Spent and exhausted, Shadow nearly fell backward onto the dirty ground, but Brett pulled him up to his feet and held him close. Shadow was in a haze, wondering if he actually did what he did or if it was all a fantasy. Brett's soft lips on his answered that question.

"The show's over!" a gruff voice yelled. "Get your asses inside before they decide to charge you a second cover charge." Shadow heard the crunch of footsteps on the dead grass come closer. "Brett, what do you think you're doing?"

Brett pulled away from the kiss. He smiled at Shadow when he spoke. "I was auditioning my first cast mate."

"Well, your audition got Kenny mad. Half the fucking bar came out here to watch you two." Shadow looked at the older man addressing Brett. He wore a tight polo, pressed khaki pants, and a stern expression that hid his gentleness. "We've been banned, for now."

Brett kept his eyes on Shadow when he spoke. "Fuck him."

"I'll smooth it over tomorrow. In the meantime, put your dick away and get out of here," the man ordered. "Don't forget to take blondie here with you"

With a satisfied smile, Brett asked, "What do you say we head back to my place and continue the audition?"

"Sounds good to me." Shadow smiled back.

Brett turned his attention to the man. "We'll see you back at the house, Joe."

"Just keep it down." As Joe began stomping away, he grumbled, "Fucking whore."

BIRTH OF THE COUNTRY BOYZ

"**W**OW. THAT WAS some first meeting." Jordan shifted on the couch. "Had you gone into a sexual trance before?"

It took a moment for Shadow to respond. "Sexual trance?"

"It's what you described. When you lose yourself in the moment," Jordan explained. "It sounds like you went into a sexual trance. You were aware of everyone else around you, but you were solely focused on Brett. His pleasure and praise. You even subconsciously held back your own orgasm until he climaxed."

Shadow sounded surprised when he spoke. "Oh. I never had a name for it before."

"Billy says I do something similar when I write. I go into this trance. I'm solely focused on writing, and I'm not really aware of anything around me," Jordan mused. "He lets me be but makes sure I have something to eat or drink on hand until I come out of it. Then he'll wrap me up in his arms and snuggle me."

Jordan wasn't prepared for Shadow's next statement. "You really love him."

"What? Of course I do," Jordan responded, a little offended that his feelings for Billy were being questioned.

Shadow's voice was apologetic. "I didn't mean to offend you. It's that when I see you and Billy together in pictures or videos, you can see he's all about you. You seem to distance yourself from him. You move away, try not to look at him."

"I don't," Jordan defended. He thought about it for a moment. They had been at a small party at Lexi's house recently. Billy would put his arms around him, or hold his hand and he'd move away. "Wait, I do. I never realized it before. I don't only do it in public, but when we're in private settings, too."

Shadow's voice interrupted Jordan's revelation. "A little advice, Billy isn't the type of guy you can only love in private. He lived that life once and, well, you know what happened."

"I can't believe I've been doing that to him." Jordan shook his head in disbelief. "Thank you for telling me that."

Jordan heard the smile in Shadow's voice. "You're welcome. Billy deserves happiness. He deserves you. All of you."

"Hey, I have a question," someone Jordan assumed was Shadow's husband chimed in. "What's it called when he goes all feral and sex-crazed?"

Shadow let out an audible sigh. "That's called being horny, dear."

"That sounds more primal." Jordan laughed, feeling more at ease. "Sometimes when I stimulate Billy…" Jordan caught himself. "Never mind."

Jordan hated how Shadow was able to finish his thought. "His eyes glaze over and he becomes this beast in the sheets."

"That's you, sweetie. I have the nail marks on my back to prove it," the unknown voice said without a hint of shame.

Shadow groaned. "That was more information than I wanted to give."

"We're getting off course here," Jordan said, regaining control of the interview. "Why did you lie about your name to Brett?"

Jordan heard Shadow take in several deep breaths. "I honestly don't know. I think it's because deep down, I knew I needed to leave who I was behind. I needed to find myself, define myself without all the labels of being the rich boy, the party boy, the spoiled brat."

"You were a spoiled brat," Shadow's husband grumbled loudly. "Whenever you had to share a room with your cousin, you'd lock him out of the room."

Shadow sniped back. "We have six bedrooms in this house? Why did I have to share a bedroom with my younger cousin?"

"Two of the bedrooms were being used by me and my dad, and one was being used as storage while we renovated the house and barn, remember?" Shadow's husband shot back. "Now, back to your interview."

Jordan let out a laugh. "You two seem so perfect for each other."

"Thanks. It was a long road to get here," Shadow responded. "To finish answering your question, I wanted to leave who I was behind and redefine myself. I was hurting and being someone else seemed like a good solution to numb the pain."

Jordan thought for a moment. "Didn't Brett suspect you might have come from money?"

"No. I told him I was using a friend's car and staying at a friend's place. He assumed I was a kept boy, and I didn't correct him." There was hurt in Shadow's voice. "I spent most of my free time with him, only going back to my house to get clothes or money. Joe didn't seem to mind having me around. I think he liked it. I was a buffer between him and Brett."

Jordan grabbed his tablet and scrolled through his questions. "Joe and Brett were business partners, and all of you lived and filmed at Joe's house, right?"

"They were business partners by convenience," Shadow answered. "Joe came from old Southern money and that money was running dry. It didn't matter who you were, what happened, or what you needed, Joe was there to help. That's how Joe and Brett got tangled together.

"The story I was told was that Brett was a mechanic at a local garage. The owner's scrawny son came back from college to work the front desk. He came back filled out and sexually aware." Shadow laughed. "Brett, being the horn dog he was, couldn't resist the fresh meat."

Jordan nodded. He knew in the gay community a fresh face was like throwing chum in shark-infested waters. "He gave the owner's son a lube job, didn't he?"

"Several." Shadow chuckled. "The owner stopped by with a customer to check on his son and caught them. Brett had the boy's legs up in the air in the backseat of the customer's SUV when they walked in on them. Joe happened to be the customer."

Jordan's eyes went big. "Holy shit."

"Yeah, Brett was fired on the spot, and, of course, he was renting his trailer from the owner." Shadow chuffed. "Luckily, Joe didn't mind having his backseat used for a sexual liaison and felt bad for them both. Brett moved into Joe's house that same day."

Jordan sat his tablet aside. "Why were they reluctant business partners?"

"Joe's place was in the country, and when I say in the country, I mean it was a forty-minute drive to the closest town, mainly down dirt roads. He lived on several acres of land that was covered in pine trees." Shadow paused in thought. "I remember him telling me he had his property rezoned as a tree farm so he could get a break on his property taxes."

Jordan blurted out, "What?"

"There were a lot of shady things that went on in that house," Shadow responded. "Anyways, Joe needed help keeping his old house up, and Brett knew how to do the work. The problem was that they didn't like each other much. Actually, they didn't like each other at all, but they were cordial to each other. They were all each other had."

Jordan steered with his next question. "How did the Country Boyz site come into play?"

"Brett wanted out of Joe's house and was looking to make some quick money," Shadow explained. "He

found the cam sites and started making a little money. The cam fans inflated his ego, and he came up with the idea of starting his own site. How he talked Joe into it, I don't know."

Jordan decided to ask the one question that had been gnawing at him. "Why did you cut your family out of your life?"

"I didn't." Shadow's answer wasn't what Jordan expected. "My parents were fine with me staying down there, where I wasn't such a public embarrassment and off the radar. Sure, they limited my access to my trust fund, but they figured I'd come to my senses one day." Jordan heard Shadow's husband snort with laughter. "I asked you to be here to listen. Not make commentary."

Jordan smiled at hearing their little squabble. It reminded him of how he and Billy were. "Okay, Brett and Joe are starting a porn site. You became the first member of the cast, but you can't make a site with just two people. When did the other boys join in?"

"To be fair, they tried. Joe and Brett had no idea what they were doing." Jordan could almost hear Shadow roll his eyes. "They didn't know how to edit, light the actors. They got expensive cameras that weren't worth shit. The videos, for the most part, were shit. Yet they made money."

Jordan begrudgingly admitted, "I watched Billy's first video. It wasn't good. You could barely see what was going on."

"Yet it was one of the highest viewed videos," Shadow said, exasperated. "Anyways, to answer your question, we filmed content while we were looking

for others to star on the site. Honestly, I didn't think they'd get it off the ground, not even after I made my first video."

6

LIGHTS! CAMERA! ACTION!

SHADOW WAS FILLED *with nervous excitement, sitting on the bed in a tight tee and baggy shorts. Brett sat beside him in his trademark athletic shirt and tight jeans, arrogantly smiling at the camera Joe had pointed at them. This was going to be Shadow's introduction on the site, and he couldn't wait.*

Joe fumbled with the camera until he finally figured out which button to hit to start recording. He cleared his throat, then said, "Hey, everyone. Brett has brought us someone we hope to see coming back to shoot with us." Joe zoomed in on Shadow. "Introduce yourself to the people. Tell us about yourself."

"Hi, I'm Shadow." He waved to the camera. "I'm a hundred and forty pounds. I'm twenty years old. I'm versatile. I like fast cars, hot men, and big dicks."

Joe zoomed out, so it showed both Shadow and Brett. "Brett's a hot man with a big dick."

"And I drive a fast car." Brett winked at the camera.

Joe zoomed out a bit more to get the full bed in the shot. "Brett is really big. Do you think you can handle all that cock?"

"I think so," Shadow said with a giggle.

Then Joe said, "You seem a bit nervous."

"I am, a little," Shadow lied. Joe had been filming them fucking for the past two weeks to get him comfortable in front of the camera. "This is my first time in front of a camera."

Joe made his voice warm and friendly. "Don't worry. Brett, here, is a pro in front of the camera. Why don't you two pretend I'm not here and have a little fun?"

"Sounds good to me," Brett said, putting his arm over Shadow's shoulder.

Shadow looked at Brett with sinful innocence. He liked sex with Brett, but the idea of having it on camera for millions to watch sent his heart racing. "Sounds good to me, too."

Brett pulled him close. Shadow turned on the bed as he leaned in and put an arm around Brett. It looked like his body trembled from nervousness, but it was from the excitement of being filmed. Brett's lips pressed to his. Shadow parted his lips slightly, letting Brett's tongue slip in. Shadow relaxed, letting himself lose himself in the moment.

Brett's hand moved up and under Shadow's shirt. He shivered from the touch. He loved the feel of Brett's rough, calloused hands on his skin. Shadow massaged Brett's hard cock through his jeans. He felt the familiar length and hardness throbbing under his fingertips.

Brett pulled up at the hem of Shadow's shirt, forcing them to break the sensual kiss. Shadow used the moment to pull Brett's shirt off and toss it to the side. He fought the

34

urge to throw Brett down on his back and rip his jeans off. Brett kissed him, sucking on Shadow's lower lip before slipping his tongue into Shadow's moaning mouth.

They fumbled opening each other's pants. Shadow moved off the bed to let his shorts slip down his narrow hips. Stepping out of the shorts, Shadow began kissing down Brett's smooth chest. Brett leaned back on his elbows to let him kiss along his flat stomach.

Shadow sat back on his heels between Brett's outstretched legs. He grabbed the top of Brett's jeans. Brett raised his hips, and Shadow clumsily pulled them off. Shadow took a moment to enjoy the view of his new lover laying back on the bed, naked and exposed for anyone willing to pay $19.99 a month to watch.

Shadow's eyes traveled up past Brett's hard ten-inch cock to his naturally taut stomach. He took a moment to take in the lock tattooed over his heart. Then he looked up to see Brett looking down at him with a smug Cheshire cat grin. He winked at Shadow.

"I think Shadow has gotten over his nervousness," Brett said for the camera.

Shadow got up on his knees and spread Brett's legs wider. With one hand stroking the monster cock, Shadow began licking Brett's balls. Taking one ball in his mouth, he lavished it with caressing swipes of his tongue before giving the other ball the same treatment.

Shadow felt a strange euphoric state taking over him. Rising up farther, he licked up Brett's cock, swirling his tongue over the tip like it was an ice cream cone. He angled Brett's dick down. After weeks of practice, Shadow was able to take about eight inches orally.

"*Oh, yeah.*" *Brett tossed his head back. "We definitely need to have him back. Fuck. He can suck some dick."*

The praise did something to Shadow. He worked Brett's cock furiously in his mouth, trying to get those last two inches down to see what praise he would then earn. He felt Brett's hand running through his hair. Shadow groaned. He felt his cheeks warm with lust and desire.

"Damn, I need to see if his ass is as sweet as his mouth." Brett sat up. He pulled Shadow to his feet and onto the bed. Brett pushed him down onto his back. "I love me some pretty boys."

Shadow gasped at the feel of Brett's warm mouth sur-rounding his six-inch hard-on. Instinctively, he thrust his hips up into Brett's mouth, letting him slip a hand under him and a finger between his cheeks. Brett began stroking his hole while he slurped down Shadow's dick.

Shadow was lost in pleasure as Brett lifted Shadow's legs up. Pulling off Shadow's cock, he pressed Shadow's legs to his chest, curling him into a ball. Brett's tongue snaked its way down Shadow's cock, past his balls to his smooth hole.

"Oh, God," Shadow moaned, feeling Brett's tongue dance around his skin. Shadow grabbed his legs and pulled them back farther. Brett started flicking his tongue at Shadow's hole. Shadow let out a groan of delight before gasping from the sudden pleasure of Brett's tongue dashing in and out of him.

Brett licked his way back up to the tip of Shadow's dick. Sitting back on his heels, Brett kept Shadow's legs pressed to his chest. He grinned down at Shadow and said, "That ass is as sweet and juicy as a watermelon." Brett tapped

his dick against Shadow's ass. "Are you ready for this big ole cock, boy?"

"Hell, yes," Shadow growled.

Brett pressed his cock into Shadow. He watched his cock slide effortlessly into Shadow. "He's a keeper. He can take some dick." Brett laughed when he was balls deep in him. Putting his hands on either side of his head, Brett leaned forward and kissed Shadow.

Shadow felt every inch of Brett's cock slowly invading, then withdrawing inside him. Brett pulled away from the kiss. Brett rotated his hips. Shadow felt that familiar tingling warmth spread through his body. Brett's cock began rapidly slicing into him.

"Fuck me. Fuck me," Shadow panted. "Give me that big dick."

Brett raised back onto his knees. He held Shadow's legs by the ankles in the air. "Tight fucking ass," Brett grunted, slamming his cock into Shadow.

"Fuck me," Shadow repeated, one hand going to his cock. Brett pulled out until just the tip was in Shadow, then slammed back in. Brett repeated the process. Shadow clawed the bed with his free hand. He moaned, "Stop teasing me."

Brett began rapidly thrusting into Shadow. "You want that dick, boy? I'll give you that dick alright." Brett pulled out of Shadow. He rolled Shadow onto his stomach. He smacked Shadow's ass. "Get up on all fours."

"Come on. Fuck me like you mean it," Shadow called back over his shoulder as he got up on all fours. He felt Brett line up with him. Once he felt the head of Brett's dick at his entrance, Shadow pushed back until Brett was halfway in. He rolled his back as he moaned, "Oh, yeah."

Brett playfully smacked Shadow's ass. "Eager little bottom." He gripped Shadow by the right hip, while he used his other hand to ease his cock the rest of the way into Shadow. "A guy could get used to feeling this hole on his cock."

Brett began pounding into Shadow. After a few minutes, Shadow began meeting Brett's thrusts, needing to feel Brett deeper in him. He reached under himself and stroked his cock. Brett gave his other cheek a slap. Shadow arched his head back in a growling moan at the pleasurable pain.

"Fuck, this ass is tight." Brett slapped Shadow's ass. "Damn, he's milking me with his ass."

Shadow began bouncing back harder. He felt a haze drift over his mind. The urge to feel Brett get off surged through him. Getting Brett off was the only thing that mattered, whether it was on him or in him. His own orgasm didn't matter. It was all about Brett and his pleasure.

"Damn." Brett pulled out of Shadow and began furiously stroking his dick. Shadow rolled over onto his back, beating his own meat. Brett thrust his hips forward, coating Shadow's cock and balls with his white, sticky seed. "Fuck!" he yelled through clenched teeth.

Set off by Brett's orgasm, Shadow's balls tingled and drew up. Using Brett's load as lube, he pumped his cock until his own load shot across his chest. He jerked and spasmed while grunting and groaning. His head raised up and slammed back into the bed. His body tensed up before the final shot landed on his belly.

"Now that was a show," Joe said from behind the camera.

Brett fell down beside Shadow and began playing with the strings of cum on his chest. "That was amazing."

"What do you think, Shadow?" Joe asked. "Do you think you'll come back to shoot some more videos?"

Shadow looked at Brett's grinning face, then at the camera. "Most definitely."

RECIPROCATION

"**W**ow." Jordan leaned back. "I wish I could see that scene. There aren't many Country Boyz videos still floating out there."

Shadow let out a humorless laugh. "That's because Joe and Brett didn't know what they were doing, remember? Most of the videos are lost to memory."

"Could you elaborate?" Jordan asked, intrigued.

Shadow snorted. "They didn't pay someone to host the site. They did it themselves, in Joe's house on regular home computers. They burned out, shorted out. They got whoever was cheapest to come out and fix the problems."

"The hard drives and content were lost," Jordan clarified.

Shadow scoffed. "All the pictures we took were free downloads on the site, so they were scattered across the web. Toward the end is when Brett started uploading portions of our videos to the various sites to try and get more traffic, but it was over by then."

40

"Did you believe in the Country Boyz site?" Jordan leaned forward, staring at the black square like he would a person.

There was a moment of silence before Shadow answered. "I believed in Brett. I believed in the idea. I didn't believe that Brett could pull it off."

"Then why did you do it?" Jordan asked, curiously.

There was a long pause before Shadow finally answered. "I loved him and wanted to support him. I sort of got lost in the thrill of the idea that people would be watching me have sex."

"Did he…" Jordan stopped himself from asking the question.

Shadow finished the question. "Did he love me? Yes, he did. He just loved his dream more."

"Is that why you left?" Jordan probed.

Jordan heard Shadow shifting in his chair. "Let's come back to that, okay?"

"Okay, how was your relationship with the other Country Boyz?" Jordan braced himself for the answer. He didn't want to know about Billy and Shadow's relationship, but he had to know.

Jordan heard the smile in Shadow's voice. "Mario and I were best friends. He's the one who helped keep Country Boyz afloat by having us escort. We had quite a few high-profile clients, and before you ask, no, I won't name them."

"Understood." Jordan nodded. "What about Kevin and Keith?"

Shadow sounded hesitant when he spoke. "They really weren't part of the group. Keith was straight, and Kevin was in love with him. That's why Kevin

convinced Keith to film. It was the only way he could be with Keith."

"What about Billy?" Jordan squeaked out.

Shadow's laughter shocked him. "When Billy moved in, he was so hesitant to let anyone in. It took almost two months before he warmed up to any of us. After what he had been through, I didn't blame him. That's why I knew I could trust you. Billy trusts you with his heart. That's not something he does easily."

"Really?" Jordan asked, a little shocked.

Shadow's voice grew serious. "Really. If Billy calls you a friend, he'll move Heaven and Earth for you. If he loves you, he'll live and die for you. You are one lucky man."

"I am." Jordan smiled warmly.

Shadow asked, "Does he still send money to his mother?"

"He does." Jordan couldn't hide the bitterness in his voice. "She still won't see him or accept his calls."

Shadow's voice was consoling. "She'll come around one day."

"And if she doesn't?" Jordan asked, his bitterness morphing into concern.

Jordan heard the held-back tears in Shadow's voice. "Hold Him like you're going to hold him when you tell him you can't tell him where I am."

"Will you do one thing for me?" A tear ran down Jordan's cheek. "For Billy?"

Shadow hesitantly asked, "What?"

"Will you record something for Billy? To help him to understand?" Jordan pleaded.

Shadow answered without a second thought, "Of course."

"Thank you." Jordan wiped a tear away. "It'll mean a lot to him, and to me."

Shadow sounded emotionally choked up. "Will you do something for me? For Billy?"

"Sure," Jordan said without hesitation.

Shadow let out a choked sob. "Love him the way he deserves to be loved. Freely and openly."

"I haven't been," Jordan admitted. "I will though." Jordan wiped at his watering eyes. "I love him so much."

"I know you do," Shadow sobbed. "Do you think we could pick this up tomorrow?"

Jordan nodded. "Sure."

INTERVIEW AFTERCARE

SHADOW WATCHED THE screen go blank. He hadn't expected their interview to have this effect on him. The tears from the memories Jordan and he dredged up wouldn't stop. He felt Chris's hand on his shoulder. He couldn't look at the man he was in love with, having admitted to loving two other men.

"Are you okay?" Chris asked softly.

Shadow's lips moved, but no sound came out. Finally, he was able to eke out, "How can you even look at me? I admitted to loving two other men."

"Look at me." With a gentle hand on Shadow's chin, Chris turned his lover to face him. "You told me about Brett, remember?"

Shadow closed his eyes. It hurt to look at Chris's gentle, forgiving face, etched with laugh lines. "I never told you about Billy."

"You didn't have to. I knew." Chris stroked Shadow's face. "Not Billy, specifically, but I knew someone else was in your heart along with me. That's okay. I'm sure there's room enough in there for us all."

Shadow opened his eyes to see Chris's scruffy face smiling at him. "You don't have to be here for the rest of it. If you don't want to be."

"And hear about it as second hand gossip in town?" Chris teased. "I know it's going to be rough, especially when it gets to us. That's okay. You need this, and you need me here by your side."

Shadow wiped away his tears. "I don't deserve you."

"You don't, but I deserve you," Chris joked.

Pulling Chris into a hug, Shadow laughed. The man knew how to make him smile. He wished it hadn't taken him so long to see that Chris was the right man for him. He fought it, but Chris fought harder for him. It didn't matter how many times Shadow tried to push Chris away, he pushed back harder.

"I don't tell you this enough," Shadow squeezed Chris tighter. "I love you with all of my heart."

Chris nuzzled Shadow's cheek. "You tell me it all the time. When you hold me until my tremors stop, when you wordlessly clean up my spills, and when you indulge me with my peanut butter and chocolate syrup sandwiches."

Shadow laughed. "I love how you smile when you eat them."

"See? You tell me all the time, just not with words." Chris pulled away to look at his husband.

Shadow knew the answer, but needed to hear the answer from Chris. "Do I tell them about your injury?"

45

"You sort of have to," Chris answered solemnly. "It was a hard time in our history together, but it's our history."

Shadow swallowed hard. "It's going to be hard bringing up all those memories. Are you sure you want to be here for it?"

"I was here to make them, and I'll be here for them when you have to dredge them back up." Chris took Shadow's hands. "Didn't we have this conversation before?"

Shadow bit his lip. "Yes, we're in this together. No matter what."

"That's right. Why don't you freshen up, and we can snuggle on the couch the rest of the afternoon?" Chris grinned.

Shadow rolled his eyes with a sigh. "I know what you're up to."

"What?" Chris asked innocently.

Shadow poked him in the chest. "Don't play innocent. Snuggling leads to cuddling. Cuddling leads to kissing. Kissing leads to us getting naughty and needing to take a shower after."

"The shower after is my favorite part." Chris winked at him.

Shadow sucked on his lower lip in thought. "I'll meet you on the couch."

Jordan pulled his legs up onto the couch and watched the recorded interview. It wasn't until he stopped

recording and looked at the timer that he realized the interview had gone on for two hours. Shadow had described in great detail his first encounter with Brett and the first time they filmed together.

The pointed insights into his and Billy's relationship were one thing he didn't expect from the interview. Shadow obviously kept tabs on Billy and harbored some sort of feelings for him. Jordan was doing this interview to help Billy get closure, but why was Shadow? Was he doing it in some strange attempt to get Billy?

He checked his phone. Billy had sent him pictures from their layover. The first were goofy pictures of him and Carlos that made him laugh. The last picture was of Billy making puppy dog eyes at the camera with "Miss you, Teddy Bear" written at the bottom. That one made him smile.

Billy was up in the air now, but Jordan responded.

[I miss you, too. Be good. Call me when you get a chance. I want to hear your voice.]

Jordan scrolled through his contacts. He needed to talk to someone. His old friends were nice about Billy and his relationship, but Jordan could tell they looked down on Billy and his work. His mom and dad were completely out of the question, though they loved Billy. Lexi would yell at him for following up on Shadow. Cameron was dealing with Alex. That left Drake.

As he dialed his number, his stomach twisted in a knot. The knot twisted tighter when Drake answered chipperly, "Jordan, what's up, buttercup?"

"Hey, Drake, you got a minute to talk?" Jordan asked.

Hearing how fragile Jordan sounded, Drake's tone grew concerned. "What's wrong?"

"Promise me you won't get mad?" Jordan cringed after saying the words.

Drake's voice turned stern. "What did you do?"

"Shadow," Jordan answered simply. He braced himself for the coming scolding.

Jordan could hear Drake take calming breaths before he spoke. "Jordan, Lexi told you to stop looking for Shadow. You know how much it hurts Billy every time a lead turns up a dead end."

"This is different." Jordan took a moment to gather his words.

Drake didn't give him a chance to answer. "Wait. Did you find him?"

"No, he found me." Jordan felt a chill run down his spine.

Drake asked cautiously, "Are you sure?"

"It's him. He knows the things Billy told me that only Shadow would know." Jordan felt the knot in his stomach twist tighter. "After I dropped Billy and Carlos off at the airport, I came back here and interviewed him for two hours."

Drake asked with suspicion, "Lexi and Billy don't know, do they?"

"No. I didn't want to get Billy's hopes up if it wasn't him, and I didn't want Lexi putting a stop to it," Jordan explained. "The thing is, I didn't expect it to affect me so much."

"How so?" Drake asked.

Jordan looked around at the place he shared with Billy. "Shadow kept tabs on Billy and me. He pointed out some things. Some things that really bothered me."

"Billy is not going to leave you." Drake sighed.

Jordan pulled at a stray string on his shirt. "Honestly, with the way I've treated him. I wouldn't blame him if he did."

"You treat Billy great. What are you talking about?" Drake questioned.

It hurt Jordan to say the words, but he did. "Have you ever noticed that when Billy and I are in public together, and Billy tries to touch me, I pull away?"

"I just thought you weren't into public displays of affection. A lot of people aren't," Drake commented.

Jordan sighed. "It's because subconsciously I'm scared of how people will comment about me being with Billy. And I think he's going to leave me."

"He's not going to leave you," Drake groaned.

Jordan looked at his blank computer screen. "Shadow helped me see that. That's the reason he approached me. He saw how much Billy loved me." Jordan let out a humorless laugh. "He saw in pictures what I couldn't see for myself."

"You know, when we first met Billy, we had to point out that he was dating you, right?" Drake asked.

Jordan snorted. "I was so confused because he was Billy and I was me, and he was spending all this time with me."

"He was cooking for you, cleaning for you, and snuggling in bed with you," Drake said with a smile in his voice. "He even stuck up for you at Lexi's party, remember?"

Jordan smiled to himself. "Yeah, I honestly never had someone like Billy make me feel so seen and loved. He believed in me. He takes me out of my comfort zone, and I am so much better for it."

"Jordan, where are you going with this?" Drake asked, confused.

Jordan thought for a moment. "I don't know. I do know I need to go shopping tomorrow for something."

PHONE SEX

JORDAN RAN HIS hand over the spot in the bed where Billy would be. The place was too quiet without Billy. The bed was too big without him. He and Billy had spent nights apart with their work, but this was the first night he really needed Billy there with him.

Jordan's phone rang. He saw Billy's picture flash across the screen and he smiled. "Hey, Billy," he answered.

"Hey, Teddy Bear, did I wake you?" Billy asked.

Jordan sat up in the bed. "No, I was just laying here, missing you."

"Aw, I miss you, too, Teddy Bear," Billy crooned into the phone. "I can't wait until you get here."

Jordan looked over at the spot Billy would have been in. "I wish Cameron and I didn't have to postpone getting there."

"Me, too, Teddy Bear," Billy pouted. "You'll be here soon enough, though."

The guilty knots in Jordan's stomach twisted. It was time to start unraveling them, one at a time. "Billy, I'm sorry for not being the boyfriend you deserve. I'm going to start being the man you deserve. I promise."

"What are you talking about?" Billy asked, confused. "You're the best boyfriend ever."

Jordan wanted to feel better hearing what Billy said, but couldn't. "Billy, it's come to my attention that in public I shy away from you." Jordan swallowed hard. "You are so proud to let the world know I'm yours, but I don't do the same for you." Jordan began getting choked up. "Billy, I love you so much."

"Hey, hey, Teddy Bear," Billy cut in. "I don't need you to do anything to show me that you love me. I know it."

Jordan chose his words carefully. "I need to do it for me. I want to love you freely and openly, not just in private."

"Does that mean we're making a video?" Billy teased with a hint of wickedness.

Jordan tried not to laugh. "We're not making a video."

"I know, but I wanted to hear you smile," Billy responded. "You do what you need to do, but know I love you no matter what."

Jordan looked longingly over at the empty side of the bed. "I wish you were here right now so I could show you how much I love you."

"Okay. Show me. What are you wearing?" Billy asked mischievously.

Jordan groaned. "Billy, we're not having phone sex."

"I know you're not wearing anything," Billy said smoothly. "Now let me do this. Put me on speakerphone, lay back, close your eyes, and let me talk. All you have to do is listen and enjoy yourself."

Jordan put the phone on speaker, then set it where Billy would be lying. Settling down into the bed, he said, "Okay."

"You're naked, sleeping in our bed," Billy began, making his voice low and sultry. "I slip in quietly and slowly pull the sheet off of you to reveal your sexy body."

Jordan chuffed, "You quiet? Me with a sexy body?"

"No commentary," Billy admonished. "Now, where was I? Oh, yeah." Billy lowered his voice. "My eyes roam over your sexy, naked body. I'm so hard knowing that you're mine. I can't help it. I have to touch you, so I know it's not a dream."

Jordan moaned at the thought. "Oh, Billy,"

"Sshh. You're not awake yet," Billy chided gently. "I run my hand up the inside of your bare leg. Can you feel my touch?"

Jordan's skin prickled at the thought of Billy touching him. His voice trembled when he answered, "Yes."

"Touching you is turning me on." Billy continued, keeping his voice low and seductive. "You're getting excited, too. I'm watching your big fat cock plump up." Sensing Jordan was about to say something, Billy quietly added, "Remember, no commentary. Now exhale."

Jordan slowly let his breath out, just loud enough that Billy could hear him. Billy continued, "Good. Now my hand is lightly petting your smooth balls."

Jordan felt a tingle run through his body. He could almost feel Billy's touch. "Then I'm going to drag just one finger up along your meaty rod."

Jordan could feel his pulse begin to race. Billy continued on, "I can't resist. I rub my hand over your furry belly. I love the way it feels in my fingers. It's so soft." Billy let out a low growl. "I don't want to stop touching you, but I can't keep my clothes on around you."

Billy made his voice as sensual as possible. "I strip naked. I'm so hard for you. Are you hard for me?"

"Yes," Jordan answered, his voice filled with lust.

Billy kept his voice sensual but made it commanding. "I want you to stroke yourself, but don't cum until I tell you. Understood?"

"Yes." Jordan grabbed the small bottle of lube they kept on the nightstand. He popped the top, then drizzled it over his shaft. After putting it back, he began slowly stroking his cock. Jordan let out a low moan. "I wish you were here, Billy."

"Sshh. Close your eyes and I am there," Billy said softly. "I lean over and lightly kiss you on the lips. Your eyes slowly open. You smile at me. Before you can ask what I'm doing, I slide on top of you and kiss you deeply. Your hands come around me to run along my strong back. At the feel of your touch, I grind into you."

Jordan slowly stroked himself; he could almost feel Billy's weight on him.

"I grind my hard cock against yours," Billy continued. "You open your mouth to say something, but I cut you off with a kiss. A deep passionate kiss."

Pre-cum dripped from Jordan's tip onto his stomach, and he let out a low moan.

"I kiss my way down your body." Billy's voice started getting huskier. "I've got to taste you. I take your cock in my mouth, and I slowly suck you down. I move up and down, with my tongue teasing the tip."

Jordan's balls began to tingle. He slowed his stroking.

"I work my way to the tip, then off your cock. I run my tongue along the underside of your shaft, down past your balls. I lift your legs up and press them into your chest. I blow a cool stream of air on your hole before I move in and slowly run my tongue in circles around your hole."

Jordan sucked on his lower lip.

"I dart my tongue in and out of you. I can't take it anymore. I have to be in you. I quickly move up your body and pin your legs to your chest." Billy let out a groan. "I kiss you hard while pushing my cock into you." Billy paused. "Can you feel it? My throbbing dick?"

Jordan whimpered, "Yes."

"My cock fits so perfectly in you. It's like it was made for me," Billy moaned. "Our tongues dance while I thrust into you over and over."

Through clenched teeth, Jordan pleaded, "Billy."

"I know you want to cum, Teddy Bear," Billy said. "I want you to cum, too, but not yet."

Jordan's body tensed. "Billy," he begged.

"Okay, Teddy Bear. Blow your load for me." Billy relented. "Blow your load, thinking of my body on

top of yours, with my cock in your ass and my tongue down your throat."

Jordan thrusted up into his pumping hand. "Billy!" he cried out. White spunk shot all over his stomach and chest. "Billy! Oh, Billy!" His body shook with the aftermath of his orgasm. "Oh, Billy," Jordan sighed.

"How are you feeling, Teddy Bear?" Billy asked wickedly.

Jordan took several deep breaths. He flicked the evidence of his orgasm onto his stomach. "Where did you learn that?"

"You don't live with a writer and not pick up some tricks," Billy teased. "That was fun."

Jordan settled in the bed. "It was. It makes me miss you more, though."

"You're not going to tell me what these secret projects are, are you?" Billy asked.

Jordan swallowed hard. "Lexi doesn't even know what I'm doing."

"Jordan!" Billy scolded, then reluctantly admitted, "Better to ask for forgiveness than permission."

Jordan thought to himself, *Will you forgive me, though?* Jordan felt a new knot tighten in his stomach. "I should let you get to sleep. Aren't you filming tomorrow?"

"Yeah, and Carlos locked me out of his room so I can't sneak in and cuddle him," Billy pouted.

Jordan laughed. "You'll have your Teddy Bear soon. Get some rest, Billy. I'll talk to you tomorrow. Good night, Billy."

"Sweet dreams, Teddy Bear," Billy said sweetly before ending the call.

Jordan lay there, his spunk drying on his skin. He closed his eyes and wondered, *Will I be Billy's hero or villain in this story?*

10

PILLOW THOUGHTS

LYING IN THE bed with Chris's head resting on his chest, Shadow couldn't sleep. His mind was racing with what he should and should not tell Jordan tomorrow. Jordan knew about Chris now. Shadow wasn't sure if he was willing to share that story with the world. It was theirs, as ugly and beautiful as it was.

Running his hand down Chris's back, Shadow closed his eyes. It seemed so long ago that he and Chris had found each other again, although it had only been a few years. Jaded, Shadow had arrived broken-hearted from leaving Brett and longing for Billy after Shadow had sent him away. The last thing he had expected or wanted was to see Chris. His first love. The man who had disappeared on him.

The sun was setting when Shadow pulled up in his car to the old family getaway. The air was crisp. The leaves were beginning to change. Here he could be isolated and deal with his feelings for both Brett and Billy. Here he'd be away from his family that lectured and scolded him for taking so long to come to his senses.

Shadow got out of the car, slung his bag over his shoulder, and made his way up the wrap-around porch. He noticed the hanging plants, brown and wilting, in desperate need of attention. He went over to the third flower pot on the ground from the door. Whatever had been put in there had long since withered away.

Lifting the pot, he took the spare key it hid. He looked out into the yard. The green grass swayed in the cool wind. He noticed a worn path from the house to the converted barn in which they kept their snowmobiles and ski equipment. He doubted that he'd make use of any of it.

Shadow nearly jumped out of his skin when he heard a stern voice behind him ask, "Can I help you?"

Turning around, he saw a young man about his age with shaggy brown hair. The man was wearing a tee advertising a local restaurant and worn, faded jeans. He was a little plumper than Shadow remembered, but he knew the man. The man looked hard at Shadow. His face brightened. "Shadow? Is that you?"

"Chris?" Shadow dropped his bag and hugged the man. "What are you doing here?"

Shocked by the embrace, Chris returned the hug reluctantly. "Didn't your father tell you? I'm the caretaker."

"Wait? You live here?" Shadow asked, pulling away. "I thought you went away to college."

Chris took a step back. He looked at Shadow in confusion. "When was the last time you spoke to your parents? Do they even know you're here?"

"Sort of. Can we go inside? It's been a long drive." Shadow grabbed his bag.

Awkwardly, Chris shuffled over to the door and held it open. "Of course."

"Is your dad here, too?" Shadow asked, stepping into the house. Dropping his bag by the couch, he plopped down. He watched Chris limp from the door, then noticed him flexing his left hand. "Did you hurt yourself?"

Chris fell onto the couch. He let out a grunt as he settled in. "That's why I asked when the last time you spoke to your parents was." He shifted on the couch. "My father moved to Florida two years ago. He couldn't take the winters anymore."

"Okay, but I saw you limping and your hand," Shadow pointed out.

Trying to get comfortable, Chris shifted on the couch again. "I hurt my back carrying some big pieces of wood from a tree Dad and I cut down." Chris rolled his eyes. "I tried to be this big badass. The next morning, I got out of bed and nearly fell over."

"Oh, my God! Are you okay?" Shadow asked, then immediately regretted it. "Stupid question."

Chris smiled. "I get that question a lot. I was on a cane for a couple of months. The injury caused nerve damage on my left side. I have problems walking, and my left hand doesn't always work right."

"Your dad left you here alone like this?" Shadow asked, shocked.

60

Chris narrowed his eyes at Shadow. "He took me to all my doctors' appointments for injections and helped me get off my cane. He did a lot for me, and I'm not feeble. Sure, I have problems with stairs and I might spill a little, but I can do things on my own."

"I'm sorry, I didn't mean to…" Shadow reached over and carefully took Chris's hand. "I'm an idiot. My dad didn't get a chance to tell me anything. When I called him, we got into a fight because… Never mind. I just told him I was coming up here and hung up on him. I've been ignoring his calls since."

Chris looked at Shadow's hand holding his. "It's strange he didn't call and tell me you were coming."

"I didn't specifically tell him I was coming here," Shadow answered sheepishly. "I may have given him the impression I was heading to California."

Chris looked at him in confusion. "Why would you do that? You know I have to tell him you're here, right?"

Shadow pulled his hand back. "I'll call him. Tomorrow. I promise." He felt guilty about what he was going to ask next. "Do you mind if I grab something to eat? I didn't think about getting food until I was on the road here."

"If you want something besides snacks or frozen meals to eat, you'll probably have to head out with me to the diner in town," Chris answered, embarrassed. "I don't cook much anymore."

Shadow was about to ask why he had stopped cooking, then looked at Chris's hand. "Oh, right. Well, I plan on being here for a bit, if you don't mind. I can help with the cooking and anything that you need me to."

"Does that include giving me a bath?" Chris asked with a smirk

Without even thinking, Shadow answered, "Yeah, totally. Anything you..." He saw Chris's grin. He playfully smacked Chris on the arm. "You asshole. You know I totally would have done it."

"Would you really? You're such a freak." Chris laughed until he saw Shadow shrink into the couch. Concerned, he asked, "Are you okay?"

Shadow shook his head. His voice went soft and was filled with hurt. "Can we not talk about that right now?"

"Yeah, anything you want." Chris wiggled his fingers before reaching out and putting his hand on Shadow's knee. "If you want to freshen up, you can use my shower down here. I normally have more notice to get the upstairs ready for everyone."

Shadow lifted his arm and smelled himself. "I am a bit ripe. You don't mind?"

"Your smell? Yes. You using my shower? No. I'll get you some fresh towels." Chris struggled to get up from the couch.

Shadow got up. "I'll go get my things. I guess I can crash on the couch until I get upstairs livable."

"That bed your parents put in there is huge. We can share it." Chris winked at Shadow. "Just make sure you control yourself."

Shadow looked at him incredulously. "Excuse me, but you were the one who couldn't keep his lips off mine."

"What can I say? I kissed a boy, and I loved it." Chris grinned. "I know I said differently at the time, but you were my first kiss."

Shadow blushed. "I knew that. You were my first kiss, too." Shadow let out a laugh. "If you hadn't taught my cousin how to unlock my door, you might have been my first something else, too."

"Oh, really?" Chris's grin grew bigger.

Shadow rolled his eyes. "Don't flatter yourself. You were the only male I wasn't related to that was available."

"Still am." Chris gave a little wink before heading over to the downstairs suite.

Shadow kissed the top of Chris's head. He smiled at Chris stirring in his arms. Shadow pulled him closer. Careful not to wake Chris, Shadow whispered, "Everything I went through with Brett and Billy was to bring me back to you."

"Did you say something?" Chris asked sleepily.

Shadow stroked his back. "No, I was just thinking."

"Don't do that." Chris snuggled closer to Shadow.

Shadow closed his eyes with a smile. "It was about you."

"Oh, that you can do." Chris yawned.

11

CHRIS CALLS JORDAN

"**Y**ES, DRAKE, IT'S okay. We can go another day…" Jordan trailed off when he saw the incoming video call on his computer. "Let me call you back." Jordan sat down on the sofa and answered the call. He expected a blank screen, but what he got was a scruffy, brown-haired guy looking at the computer, bewildered.

The man tapped randomly at keys. "Did I do it right? Is this it?"

"Hello?" Jordan asked.

Shocked, the man looked up, into the camera. "Can you see me?"

"Um, yeah." It took a moment, but Jordan recognized the voice. "Are you Shadow's husband?"

Chris looked guiltily into the camera. "Yeah, I didn't think you'd answer. I was going to leave you a voicemail."

"That's not how video calls work." Jordan looked at him suspiciously. "Shadow doesn't know you're on the computer with me, does he?"

Chris shook his head. "No. He's in town doing errands."

"You shouldn't be on camera with me. I shouldn't be talking to you," Jordan blurted out in a panic. "If Shadow finds out, he'll end these interviews."

Chris put up a hand. "I won't let him. He needs this, and I need to tell you about the Shadow I know. It feels weird calling him Shadow. I know him as—"

"Stop!" Jordan cut him off. "First off, no real names. Second, could you turn your camera off? Shadow and I agreed there'd be no faces."

Chris studied the screen. "Right. How do I do that? Shadow handles all the computer stuff. Wait, I think I got it." Chris's camera went dark. "Can you see me?"

"It's off." Jordan relaxed. He tried to fix his hair in the camera, but gave up. "Are you ready for me to record?"

Jordan heard Chris settling in. "Yeah, let's do this."

"Okay." Jordan pressed the record button. "Okay, Shadow's husband. You wanted to tell me about the Shadow you know. Tell me."

It took a moment for Chris to start. "Shadow saved my life when he showed up on my doorstep. Well, technically, it was his father's doorstep. You see, I took over as the caretaker of the place when my father couldn't take the winters here anymore. He wanted me to go with him because he was scared for me. What was I going to do in Florida? Carve palm trees?"

"You're rambling," Jordan cut in, smiling.

Chris exhaled loudly. "Yeah, I do that when I'm nervous or have a bad nerve day. You see, I have a back injury. I hurt my back trying to carry pieces of wood that were too heavy and didn't get it looked at right away."

"I see." Jordan pulled his legs up on the couch. "How did Shadow save you? Did he take you to the doctor? Nurse you back to health?"

Chris laughed. "Sort of. You see, I have nerve damage on my left side. I have problems with my left hand. It doesn't always do what I tell it to do, and my left leg is the same way. I can't stand for long periods of time. Certain floors are extremely hard for me to walk on and stairs are nightmares for me."

"That's horrible," Jordan said, concerned.

Chris's voice went somber. "The worst part was I had to give up my woodworking because I couldn't trust myself with the tools. I ate off plastic plates and drank out of plastic cups because I'd drop things. I was slowly spiraling into a dark place. I only left the house when I had to, and I avoided everyone when I did."

The smile returned to Chris's voice. "Then I found Shadow on the front porch. It was the first time I had smiled in a long time. I was pretty broken when he showed up. He never treated me like I was broken. He learned my limitations, pushed me to test them, and came with me to my doctor's appointments."

Chris laughed. "First, the doctor lectured me about losing weight and taking my medications. Then Shadow let into me. When he was done, the

doctor told me I had better listen to my boyfriend. I don't know which was funnier. The look of shock on Shadow's face when the doctor said it, or the look on the doctor's face when I said, 'He's not my boyfriend. We just sleep together every night.'"

"You did not," Jordan laughed.

Chris let out a hearty laugh. "I did."

"You remind me of Billy. He'd do something like that," Jordan mused.

"I'd like to meet him one day. You, too." Chris said wistfully. "You know I'm going to get Shadow to reconnect with Billy so I can."

Jordan sucked his lower lip. "Thanks, but I have to respect Shadow's wishes."

"I don't," Chris scoffed. "I married him. I can do whatever I want."

Jordan held in a laugh. "Tell me more about Shadow."

"When I have my bad nerve days, my head is all scrambled, and I can't focus on anything. He'll stop whatever he's doing and hold me," Chris continued. Jordan could tell he was silently crying. "He makes me the best peanut butter and chocolate syrup sandwiches.

"Shadow never makes me feel bad about spilling something or dropping something," Chris continued. "He simply cleans it up and acts like it was something normal. He drags me out to do these walks in the woods that I love going on. He makes me do my exercises that I can't stand but love doing with him." Chris began to get choked up. "He got me back to woodworking. He got me my art back."

Jordan felt a connection with Chris. "I know what it feels like to lose your gift like that and then find it again. Billy did that for me."

"It sounds like we have ourselves some pretty special guys. They're our muses," Chris said reflectively. "I never thought of him like that. I married my muse."

The words hit Jordan hard. "When did you guys fall in love?"

"I don't know for him, but for me, it was the first time I saw him." There was a smile in Chris's voice when he spoke. "We were fifteen. My father and I were just starting the renovations. We were staying in the house when Shadow and his family came to visit. His uncle's family came as well.

"He was the most beautiful boy I had ever seen." Chris chuckled. "He knew it, too. He was also an arrogant fuck. Wanted his own room. He kept locking his thirteen-year-old cousin out of the bedroom. Of course, I showed the kid how to pick the lock."

Chris paused in thought. "You know, if I hadn't taught him that, Shadow wouldn't have gotten mad and wanted to go for a walk in the woods, and I wouldn't have had to go with him.

"Wow," Chris said after a moment. "Anyways, Shadow was being a rude-ass, spoiled brat. I hit him with a snowball. He hit me back with one. The snowball fight lasted until I finally tackled him." Chris laughed softly. "I was on top of him, face to face. I looked into his eyes and he looked into mine. I had no choice. I kissed him."

Jordan put a hand on his heart. "That's so sweet."

"Not really," Chris said. "He kissed me back, but he also shoved snow down the back of my pants."

Jordan covered his mouth to keep from laughing. "That's, forgive me, cold."

"It was, but after that, it was really hot," Chris said impishly. "We would find little places to hide and make out until our lips were raw. Every time he came back, we picked up where we left off. Eventually."

Jordan cocked his head. "Eventually?"

"Yeah, after each visit, we'd tell each other that was the last time. Then he'd come back." Chris's voice went nostalgic. "There'd be a look or accidental touch."

Jordan thought about Billy. It only took a look or a touch to get them going. "Then you'd be all over each other."

"We thought we were being so discreet, but it was so obvious. That's why they spent so much time here. His father liked me. He knew Shadow and I were an item and liked how Shadow was when we were together." Chris took a deep breath and let it out slowly. "That's why when I hurt my back, I asked his father to tell Shadow I left for college. Everyone looked at me with pity in their eyes. I didn't want to see that in his eyes."

Jordan unconsciously hugged himself. "Do you think he would have?"

"I know now he wouldn't have. He would have stayed and taken care of me." Chris let out an audible sigh. "The way I was then, when I was hurt, I would have pushed him away."

Jordan held himself tighter. "You were in a dark place. I get it."

"I was, but the moment I saw him again… I've gone off topic." Chris stopped himself. "What I wanted to tell you is that Shadow is going to tell you about the boy he was, but I wanted to tell you about the man that he became. He's caring. Thoughtful. He loves to cook. He'll spend hours on his plants. We have these bright red begonias hanging on our front porch, and the Wandering Jew plants he has by our front door are such a deep rich purple with sparkling silver. I wish you could see them."

Jordan smiled. "Maybe one day I will."

"Maybe." Chris swallowed hard. "There are two questions you should ask Shadow. Ask him how Billy got his break and ask him about our second kiss out in the snow."

Jordan looked at the screen, puzzled. "Okay, but won't he suspect something if I ask him about the kiss?"

"He will." There was mischief in Chris's voice. "I can't wait to see his face when you ask him that one."

FLIRT FIGHTING

SHADOW SAT IN his car, mentally going over his list of errands. He had picked up Chris's medication, gone to the bank, and gotten the groceries. He had resisted the urge to stop and peruse the flowers. He didn't have time. He needed to get home and make sure Chris did his exercises before their interview with Jordan. Putting the car in gear, he started for home.

Home, he thought. *When did I start thinking of our place as home? When did I start thinking of it as our place?*

Shadow smiled when he realized when the exact moment was. He'd been at the house for a month. He had cleaned and scrubbed the upstairs, but he was still sharing a bed with Chris. He had gone with Chris to his doctor's appointment, and they had fought afterward. Making up started them on their path.

Chris's doctor pounced on the opportunity to share what Chris was doing, or rather, what Chris wasn't doing, with someone. He wasn't taking his medication. He wasn't doing his exercises. He wasn't losing weight. He was missing appointments and had completely stopped going to physical therapy. To Shadow, it seemed as if he'd given up.

Shadow waited until they were sitting down to dinner before he confronted Chris. The sexual tension between them had been building along with their feelings for one another. It made their fight weirdly humorous now that he thought about it. They were flirt fighting. It should have been Shadow's first clue that he loved Chris.

Shadow ladled the vegetable beef stew into the bowl, then sat it in front of Chris at the table. Tersely, he said, "Here's your dinner. Tomorrow we're doing your exercises and you're going back to physical therapy."

"Thank you. It looks great. You can't make me," Chris responded just as tersely.

Shadow returned to the table with his own bowl. Gruffly, he said. "I made chocolate strawberry smoothies for dessert, and yes, I can."

"I haven't had that in ages. Thank you. What are you going to do? Bend me over your knee and spank me if I don't?" Chris asked gruffly.

Shadow blew on his food, then looked at Chris coldly. "If I have to."

"I'm not that kinky." Chris shoved a spoonful of food into his mouth.

Shadow swallowed his bite. His words came out more sexually charged than he intended. "We'll see."

"Looking forward to it," Chris said before shoving another bite into his mouth.

Their flirt fighting continued through dinner and dessert. The flirting ended when Shadow smiled smugly at Chris and told him that his medicine was blended into his smoothie. Angry, Chris stormed out of the kitchen. There was an uncomfortable silence between them for the rest of the night until they were in bed.

The moon cast the room in a soft blue hue. Shadow was lying on his side, his back to Chris. Chris was doing the same to him. He could hear Chris breathing. Shadow knew Chris was sulking. He wanted to reach out to Chris and hold him. He wanted to end the stupid fight and tell Chris he was sorry. Though, he wasn't sorry.

Shadow felt the bed shift. Chris pressed his body against his and slipped an arm around Shadow. "We shouldn't go to sleep mad."

"Why won't you do what the doctor tells you?" Shadow asked, his voice full of hurt.

Chris ran his hand over Shadow's chest. "What's the point? I'm broken, Shadow. There's no fixing me."

"You're not broken. You're injured. Maybe we can't fix you, but you can live." Shadow took Chris's hand in his.

Chris's voice cracked when he spoke. "What do I have to live for?"

"For the people that love you." Shadow rolled over, so they were facing one another. For me, *he thought.*

Chris rubbed his nose against Shadow's. "Are you going to give me something to live for?"

"I…" It hurt Shadow to admit it. "I can't. I'm broken."

Chris kissed him softly on the lips. "Then let's be broken together."

"I can't give you what you want." Shadow gave Chris's hand a gentle squeeze. Their hands were intertwined between them, his hand to Chris's heart, and Chris's hand to his.

Chris softly begged. "Then give me what you can. Let me be there for you." He stroked Shadow's hair with his other hand. "I want to stop pretending I don't hear you get up in the middle of the night crying."

"I want to stop pretending I'm not hurting." Shadow brushed his lips over Chris's. "Do you know how much it hurts to be unwanted by the man you love?"

Chris pulled Shadow on top of him. "I do." Chris slowly ran a hand down Shadow's back. "I wanted you to be my first. You can't give me that, but you can be my first since my injury."

"What if I hurt you?" Shadow asked with trepidation.

Chris slipped his hand over Shadow's ass. "You could never hurt me."

Shadow gave Chris a gentle kiss. The smoldering embers of their longing erupted into flames of passion. Their lips parted. Shadow kissed Chris hard and deep. Chris returned the kiss with the same zeal and intensity. Shadow ground his crotch into Chris. He felt Chris's hands on his ass pull him harder into him.

Pulling back from the kiss, Shadow pushed Chris's head back so his neck was exposed. He slowly dragged his tongue along the exposed skin of his left side before latching on. Shadow grazed his teeth over the tender skin while sucking on the sensitive flesh. Chris gasped. His body tensed. His fingers dug into Shadow's hard, toned ass. Shadow

pulled back with a swipe of his tongue over the soft flesh, then latched onto a spot on the other side of Chris's neck.

"Oh, my God! Shadow!" Chris cried out, arching his body up into Shadow.

Worried, Shadow pulled back. Concerned, he asked, "Did I hurt you?"

"No." Chris rolled them over so he was on top. "You brought me to life."

Shadow stroked Chris's back. "I can feel that."

"Oh, you're going to feel it," Chris growled. "First, I'm going to taste you."

Chris slipped down Shadow's body. He left a trail of kisses down Shadow's chest, down his stomach to the top of his briefs. Chris ran a hand over the hard outline of Shadow's cock. Shadow arched his hips up to let Chris pull them down. Freed, Shadow's dick thumped against his flat stomach.

Chris carefully wrapped his hands around Shadow's rod. Chris said, "You don't know how long I've wanted you like this," while stroking him.

"Probably as long as I wanted you like this," Shadow panted.

Chris licked up the length of Shadow's shaft. He kissed the tip before spreading his lips over the tip. He rubbed his tongue along the underside of the crown, then looked up at Shadow's face, illuminated in the moonlight. He watched Shadow as he easily, slowly, took Shadow's cock into his mouth.

Running his hands through Chris's hair, Shadow moaned, "Oh, Chris."

With his nose pressed into Shadow's groin, and Shadow's cock wedged in his throat, Chris moaned with

gluttonous satisfaction. Reluctantly, he pulled back until the tip rested on his tongue. Chris closed his eyes and began sucking Shadow down, running his tongue along Shadow's shaft and twisting his head as he moved up and down.

Shadow fisted Chris's hair. His toes curled at the feel of Chris's warm mouth massaging his dick. "Mm, Chris. Your mouth."

It wasn't lost on Shadow that this was the first time in a long time that the sex he was having was intimate and personal. They didn't have to worry about putting on a show for an audience. They didn't have to worry about lighting, camera angles, or retakes. It was only about them and enjoying each other.

Shadow looked down at Chris, sucking his cock. Carnal lust took him. Sitting up, he pulled Chris off his cock and slammed his mouth into Chris's. He guided Chris onto his back, then moved to strip the cartoon character boxers off of him. Tossing them aside, he buried his face into Chris's groin, swallowing the six-inch hard rod.

Chris moaned. Shadow ran a hand up his body. He brushed his fingers through Chris's soft chest hair and raked his fingers down Chris's body. He felt the shiver course through Chris's body, then flicked his tongue over Chris's tip and was rewarded with another body quake. Shadow dragged his nails along Chris's side while sucking him down.

Chris thrust his hips up while pounding the bed with both fists. "Shadow!"

Shadow took the cry as encouragement. His hands alternated running up and down Chris's sides while sucking his cock and running his tongue over Chris's crown. It wasn't until Chris was hyperventilating from the pleasure that Shadow stopped and pulled off.

76

Chris barely had time to recover before Shadow had him on his stomach, cheeks spread and tongue lapping at his hole. Chris let out a guttural groan from Shadow's tongue, flicking and swirling about. Chris could feel his body relax, could feel a desire growing that he hadn't felt since his injury.

"Fuck me, Shadow," Chris moaned, raising up on his elbows. He reached into his nightstand and pulled out a bottle of lube. He tossed it beside Shadow. "Here."

Pulling back from Chris's ass, Shadow hesitantly picked up the tiny bottle. Timidly, he asked, "Are you sure?"

"Yes," Chris growled, looking over his shoulder. Softer, he said, "Go slow. It's been a while."

Shadow popped the top and drizzled lube between Chris's cheeks. He slowly rubbed a finger around Chris's hole. Pushing the finger in, he said, "Let me know if I hurt you."

"You're not going to hurt me. It's just been a while," Chris snapped.

Shadow smacked Chris's ass before slipping in a second finger. "That's what I meant, you jerk."

"No, you didn't." Chris clenched and unclenched his hole.

Shadow poured lube on his thrusting fingers, then added a third. "Quit being a dick or you won't get mine."

"Quit being an ass and fuck mine already." Chris raised up on his knees. "Please, Shadow, I need this."

Shadow pulled his fingers from Chris and began coating his cock with lube. He pressed his dick to Chris's hole. "Relax." He heard Chris take in a deep breath and exhale. He pushed into Chris and felt him tense. "Are you okay? Does it hurt?"

"*It does,*" *Chris said through clenched teeth,* "*but in a good way. Keep going.*"

Despite his better judgment, Shadow did. Slowly, he pushed into Chris. "*Are you doing okay?*"

"*Yes,*" *Chris answered with a sigh.* "*You feel so good in me.*"

Shadow pressed his hips into Chris's ass. "*I'm all the way in. Do you need me to wait?*"

"*Fuck me already,*" *Chris ordered.*

Shadow took Chris by the hips. He pulled out about an inch and pushed back in. "*Let me know if it hurts, okay?*"

"*You don't know how good it feels,*" *Chris moaned.* "*Let's stay in this position, okay?*"

Shadow pulled out a little more, then pushed back in. "*Are you ready for me to pick up the pace?*"

"*Do it.*" *Chris spit in his hand and grabbed his cock.*

Shadow slowly picked up the pace, sliding more of his dick in and out. Chris arched his back and tossed his head back. He stroked his cock in time with Shadow's thrusts. Shadow lost his timidness and began pounding Chris with fury, bouncing off his ass with each thrust.

"*Fuck me, Shadow,*" *Chris groaned.* "*Fuck me.*"

Shadow ran a hand up along Chris's spine. He raked his nails back down, sending a tremor through Chris's body. "*That's it, loosen up for me.*" *He ran a soothing hand over Chris's back.* "*I can't believe we waited so long to do this.*"

"*Are we going to talk or are you going to fuck me?*" *Chris growled. Shadow slammed hard into Chris.* "*That's it. Fuck me like you mean it.*"

Shadow gripped Chris's hips hard, pulling him back to meet every thrust. Chris's moans and the hard slap of flesh nearly drowned out Shadow's sexual snarls. Chris's

breathing became short and ragged. His hand flew over his cock. He bit his trembling lip.

"I'm… I'm…" Chris's cock exploded all over the sheets below. Tossing his head back, he shouted, "Fuck! Fuck! Fuck!"

Shadow felt Chris tighten around his dick. He bit his trembling lower lip. His balls drew up. His body tingled with the imminent eruption. He pumped furiously into Chris. "Chris! Fuck! Chris!" Shadow's cock detonated inside of Chris. His body surged with pleasure. "Oh … fuck."

Shadow collapsed on top of Chris, his cock still pulsing its last blasts. He reached out along Chris's arms to interlace their fingers. They were both breathing heavily. Shadow kissed Chris's cheek. He smiled at the feel of Chris stirring under him. They had avoided this type of intimate touch since he arrived.

"I don't mean to ruin the moment, but I need you to get off me," Chris said reluctantly.

Shadow quickly rolled off of Chris. "Are you okay? Did I hurt you? Am I hurting you?"

"No." Chris laughed, moving to cuddle up next to Shadow. "I was lying in the wet spot. It was getting sticky and cold."

Amused, Shadow kissed the top of Chris's head. "I didn't tell you to shoot all over the bed."

"I'm just happy it was on your side and not mine," Chris mused.

Shadow's hand paused while stroking Chris's back. "Hey, wait."

"We can change the sheets in a minute. I want to enjoy this moment a little longer." Chris ran his hand up and

down Shadow's chest. "That … that was the first orgasm I've had in almost three years."

Shadow froze. "What?"

"After my injury, orgasms hurt," Chris confessed. "Then I couldn't get, you know, excited enough to have one."

Dumbfounded, Shadow said, "You mean that was your…"

"You brought me back to life." Chris turned his head and kissed Shadow on the cheek. "If you stick around, I promise I'll follow the doctor's orders."

Shadow closed his eyes. "I told you. I can't give you what you want."

"You gave me back my orgasms. Who knows what else you'll give me?" Chris reasoned softly.

Shadow pulled Chris close. "I'll stay for as long as I can."

"I'll take that." Chris strummed his fingers on Shadow's chest. "How about we change the sheets so we can get some sleep?"

Shadow pulled up to the cabin. Shaking his head, he asked himself, *Why did I fight it so much? Why didn't I see what was right in front of me the whole time?* Shadow turned off the engine. Chris appeared on the porch. Shadow smiled as he thought, *It took us a while to get here, but we got here. Didn't we?*

13

HOW BILLY GOT HIS BREAK

JORDAN SAT NERVOUSLY on the couch, watching the screen. Shadow was a few minutes late. *I wonder if his husband told him that he video-called me and that I saw his face? His husband could have told him, and he changed his mind about the interviews because he doesn't trust me.*

"Sorry I'm late," Shadow's voice came over the computer. There was a bit of merriment in his voice when he said, "I remembered why I loved my husband, and we got carried away."

Jordan smiled. "I can wait for love."

"I did," Shadow said, amused. "Is there anything you wanted to ask me off the record?"

Jordan bit his lip. "There is. I'll save it for the end. I don't want those questions to color the rest of the interview."

"That's why I chose you to do this interview," Shadow responded merrily. "You want to do it right."

Jordan smiled proudly. "Thank you. Are you ready for me to record?"

"Go ahead. I'm ready," Shadow said with determination.

Tapping the record button, Jordan began, "Talk to me about the Country Boyz site. Joe was fronting the money while you and Brett were filming the content. Two people can't film enough content to keep a site going, can they?"

"No, we couldn't," Shadow admitted. "We were bringing people back to Joe's place all the time to film. We'd find them on the apps or in the bars. We really didn't care where or who we filmed with. That was part of the lure of being with Brett. I was with him, but I got to be with all these other guys. Most of the time, we didn't know or remember their names. We made them up for the site. We didn't even have paperwork on them."

Jordan hated asking the next question. "Were you really in love with Brett, or were you in love with the life?"

"That's a fair question." Shadow conceded. His voice grew somber. "At first I was in love with the idea of Brett and the life. I did love him. I know he wanted to love me the way that I wanted, but he had a dream he loved more."

Jordan glanced over at his questions. "When did Mario, Kevin, and Keith join the operation?"

"We found Mario on the apps and met up with him at The Candy Shop." The smile returned to Shadow's voice. "Mario and I were close in age and became instant friends. He was the one that got us involved

with escorting. That's how we started making the money to pay the bills. He also was the one that opened my eyes."

Jordan leaned in. "How so?"

"After he moved in, Mario became the friend I needed. We'd talk for hours and he had me questioning my relationship with Brett and why I was doing the Country Boyz site." Shadow sounded wistful. The pain seeped into his next words. "I started booking myself escort weekends away, and heading back to the family summer house and staying there."

Jordan leaned back. "Didn't Brett or anyone suspect anything?"

"Mario probably did, but he didn't say anything." There was hurt in Shadow's voice. "By then, Kevin and Keith had joined the Country Boyz. Brett was focused on them. I really hated working with them."

Jordan cocked his head questioningly. "Why?"

"Keith would only film if Kevin was involved. Kevin was in love with Keith and didn't like other guys touching him." Shadow sighed. "With Brett and Joe focusing on them because they were popular, I felt left out. Brett barely paid me any attention."

Jordan leaned toward the screen. "What about Mario?"

"He started seeing Chris. His Chris," Shadow quickly clarified. "Then, a broken Billy showed up at the house."

Jordan's heart hurt at the thought of a broken Billy. His voice cracked when he clarified, "This was after his mother threw him out, and the man he loved at the time, Teddy, sent him away."

"Yes," Shadow answered. "I knew we'd have to talk about this, but I was hoping we'd skip over it."

Jordan admitted, "Me, too. But it's part of your story, isn't it?"

"It is," Shadow sighed.

Shadow's husband spoke up, "Go on. I'm here for you."

"I forgot your husband was here with us," Jordan said, startled. "He was so quiet."

Shadow snorted. "That's because he's exhausted. He's normally as quiet as a bomb exploding."

"Hey!" Shadow's husband shouted before acquiescing. "Okay, that's true."

A heavy sadness drifted into Shadow's voice. "For the first month or so, Billy was a zombie. He didn't talk much. He barely ate. He'd go for these long walks in the woods where he'd disappear for hours. At night we'd hear him cry himself to sleep." Jordan could almost feel Shadow staring at him intently through the camera. "Do you know what it's like when Billy cries?"

"It's like watching sunshine cry," Jordan answered.

Shadow audibly took in a deep breath and let it out. "Exactly. Brett wanted to get Billy filming right away. Joe and I stopped him. Billy wasn't in the right frame of mind to perform. I felt so bad for him. He never unpacked. All of his stuff was still in trash bags."

Shadow let out a little laugh. "Mario was living with his boyfriend. He only came to film. I had him come over while Billy was on one of his walks. We unpacked all his things and tried to make the room his. We put away his clothes and put out his knick-knacks.

84

He smiled a little when he came back, but he still wasn't the same guy that we met at The Candy Shop."

"I know how I helped him when he got like that. How did you do it?" Jordan asked, scared of the answer.

Shadow chuckled softly. "I have an idea how you do it, but Mario and I took him shopping. We snuck him out while Brett was busy filming with Kevin and Keith. He was warming up to us." Shadow let out a groan. "He was such a pain to buy clothes for. He hated everything. We finally had to steal his clothes out of the dressing room to get him to try anything on."

"He got that idea from you!" Jordan blurted out.

Shadow laughed. "I take it he did that to you?"

"Yes," Jordan growled.

Shadow tried to stifle his laughter. "I bet he got a bigger smile out of you than we did out of him."

"He did. He always makes me smile." Jordan grinned at the thought of Billy. "When did you get him back to Billy?"

Shadow sighed. "We stopped off at a toy store after. Mario wanted to get something for one of Chris's nephews. Billy wandered off. I found him by the stuffed animals, hugging a teddy bear and smiling. I had to buy it for him. That was the first night he didn't cry himself to sleep. When we peeked in on him, he was curled up with the teddy bear sleeping."

"He calls me his teddy bear." Jordan smiled. "I always wondered why. He still has a hard time sleeping unless he's curled up next to someone. He's a snuggler. Once, he broke into Carlos's hotel room in the middle of the night and climbed into bed with him."

"What did Carlos do?" Shadow's husband asked with a laugh.

"Everyone is used to sleeping with Billy tangled around them. He didn't notice until he woke up the next morning," Jordan continued, amused. "Carlos said he kissed Billy on the head, then shoved him out of the bed, and yelled at Billy to go back to his room."

Shadow's husband asked, "What's your pet name for Billy?"

"I, uh, um, don't have one for him. I sometimes call him pookie, but I don't like it. It doesn't fit him," Jordan admitted guiltily. "Billy and I started dating before we realized we were dating. It was odd and sweet."

"I'd like to hear about it, sometime, if you don't mind," Shadow's husband said with intrigue.

"One day," Shadow cut in. "We should get back to my story for Jordan's interview."

Shadow's husband grumbled, "Fine."

"Billy and I became close friends. Mario, me, and him, when Mario was free, would do all sorts of things together. I think that bothered Brett, because when Billy started filming a month or so later, he made sure Billy and I were never in a scene together," Shadow went on. "Billy became the hottest thing on the site and the most popular escort. That's when I started having feelings for Billy."

Jordan glanced at his tablet. The questions Shadow's husband told him to ask screamed at him. "How did Billy get his big break?"

"Country Boyz started getting emails about Billy," Shadow hesitantly answered. "Studios wanted to hire him for scenes. Other performers wanted to collaborate

with him. Fan content sites were becoming popular, and Billy wanted to start his own."

Feeling Shadow deflecting, Jordan rephrased his question. "Is that how Billy got his big break?"

"No, Brett told Billy that if he made a content site, he couldn't film for Country Boyz anymore. He also never told Billy about the emails asking to hire him," Shadow answered vaguely. "I found out about the emails because Brett broke his phone and he needed mine to log into the site's email. He never logged out."

Jordan pressed, "Okay, so how did Billy get his break?"

"You're going to make me say it, aren't you?" Shadow asked. "Fine. I created an email and acted as Billy's agent. I forwarded the emails from the Country Boyz site to mine and started responding. I was able to find him an exclusive one-year deal with a studio. Then I rented him an apartment. I told him it was part of the exclusive deal, but not to say anything to anyone because they didn't do that for everyone."

Jordan thought for a moment. "Why didn't you go with him?"

"Mario helped me realize that Billy didn't feel the same way I felt about him." Shadow's voice was distant. "Billy's dream was to make it in the adult film industry, and Mario helped me see that I'd be leaving a man that put me second for another man that would put me second."

Jordan could hear the pain in Shadow's voice and stated, "That's when you tricked Billy into filming with you."

"Yes," Shadow answered guiltily. "If I couldn't have Billy, at least I could experience him. Mario helped me set up cameras in the barn we had. Ones that I bought. Better ones. Then Mario helped me arrange for Brett and Joe to be gone. I told Billy the studio wanted a better video of him to decide if they really wanted to hire him. In my mind, if Billy and I filmed a scene together, he might develop real feelings for me." Shadow paused. "He didn't."

THE SCENE THAT NO
ONE EVER SAW

BILLY LOOKED AROUND the barn. "Are these our cameras?"

"Yeah," Shadow lied. "Joe and Brett got them last week, I think."

Billy sat down on one of the blanket-covered bales of hay that decorated the barn. "Okay, and you're sure Joe and Brett won't find out that we did this?"

"Chris and Mario will have them busy for hours." Shadow sat down beside Billy. "This will probably be our only chance to film this for you."

Billy shifted uncomfortably. "I know, but it feels weird doing this behind their backs. You know if I do this, Brett won't let me come back and film with you guys."

"Billy, this is your big chance. You can't hesitate." Putting a hand on Billy's knee, Shadow used the one thing he knew would convince Billy. "It's the best way to help your mother, maybe get her to talk to you again."

Billy's eyes teared up. "That's not fair."

"No, but it's the truth." Shadow turned Billy's head, so they were looking at each other. "Billy, when you leave, I want you to never look back. You have an opportunity and if you don't take it, you'll regret it."

Billy cast his eyes downward. "I'm scared I won't see you guys again."

"It's not like we don't have your number." Shadow lifted Billy's chin so their eyes met again. "We'll talk on the phone, and Mario and I will come visit once you're settled. Brett will come around eventually. Joe will understand."

Billy shook his head. "How am I going to do this without you guys?"

"I'll do whatever I can to help you." Shadow looked deep into Billy's eyes. He saw the fear overshadowing Billy's confidence. "Billy, you can do this. Be yourself, and I know you're going to be the star you want to be."

"I just don't understand how that studio got my number and offered me that contract and place to stay for a year."

"Does it matter? You have it. You signed the contract already," Shadow deflected.

Billy hugged Shadow. "You're the best friend a guy could have."

"You, too, Billy." Shadow returned the hug, feeling the sting of his words. "I'm going to miss you."

When Billy pulled away, his eyes were bright. "You promise you'll visit me?"

"Yes," Shadow lied.

Billy closed his eyes. Shadow watched Billy transform himself. They were subtle changes that only someone who knew Billy would see. A slight change in his posture

and changes in his facial expressions. Billy, the fun-loving friend, faded away, and Billy, the adult film star, appeared.

Opening his eyes, Billy said confidently and sultry, "Let's do this."

Billy leaned in. Shadow's heart pounded. They were really doing this. He pressed his lips to Billy's. They were soft and warm, like he remembered. Billy ran his hand through Shadow's short, blond hair. Shadow felt the electricity in his touch. He leaned forward, guiding Billy to lie on his back on the bales.

Grinding his hips into Billy's gyrating groin, Shadow moaned, "Fuck, I want you, Billy."

"I need you naked, now." Billy pulled at Shadow's shirt.

Rolling off Billy, Shadow stood. Billy watched Shadow strip with lustful eyes. First his shirt off and tossed to the side. He kicked his shoes away, then undid his jean shorts. Letting them fall to the ground, Shadow stood there naked, chest heaving and cock hard.

Billy slipped to his knees before Shadow. He looked up at Shadow with carnal eyes. Leaning down, Shadow kissed him, pulling Billy's shirt off, then stood back up. With his eyes locked on Shadow's, Billy leaned forward to lick the pearl of pre-cum off the head of Shadow's dick.

Billy swirled his tongue over the crown. Shadow put a hand behind Billy's head. He ran his fingers through Billy's soft hair, then nudged him forward. He let out a groan from the feel of Billy's lips running over his cock, down his shaft to the base of his balls. Billy had his face pressed into Shadow's groin, Shadow's hard rod nestled deep down his throat.

Billy closed his eyes and pulled back to the tip. He rose up on his knees. Twisting his head, varying his bobs, Billy

began sucking Shadow in earnest. Billy's hand popped open the top of his shorts. Pushing them down past his ass, he pulled off Shadow only long enough to spit in his hand and start stroking his nearly ten inches.

Thrusting his hips forward, Shadow tossed his head back. Holding onto Billy's head, he shoved his cock down Billy's throat, then began pumping furiously into his mouth. Billy kept his body perfectly still, letting Shadow use his mouth. He looked down to see Billy watching him, eyes watering from the welcomed assault to his throat.

Shadow couldn't stand it. Billy was so beautiful, down on his knees before him, eyes watering, and cock sliding through his soft red lips. He pulled his cock free and replaced it with his mouth.

Keeping the kiss intact, Billy rose up. His hands came around Shadow to cup his ass. Billy's grip was firm but gentle. Shadow's hands wandered over Billy's strong back. Billy turned them, kicking his shoes off and stepping out of his shorts as he did.

Billy guided him back against the blanket-covered bale. Shadow kissed his way down Billy's body as he lowered himself onto the bale. He moved so he was on all fours, ass up in the air, and Billy's cock at the perfect height. Billy ran a hand down Shadow's spine, while the other hand pulled Shadow onto his dick.

Shadow nursed hungrily on Billy's cock. Tingles ran through his body from Billy's hand stroking along his back. Shadow arched his back more. Billy's hand reached down to his ass. Billy's middle finger rubbed over his hole before rhythmically tapping it.

Shadow let out a muffled moan. Billy removed his hand. Shadow heard Billy spit, then the hand returned to

rub saliva into his hole. Shadow pushed back against the exploring finger. Billy's finger slipped in up to the second knuckle. Billy's wiggling finger sent shivers through him.

"Your ass is so fucking hot." Billy's voice had lost all its youthful innocence. It was deep and manly.

Shadow pulled off Billy's dick. Looking up at him, Shadow said, "Take it." He turned around and presented his ass. Over his shoulder, he moaned, "Fuck me, Billy."

"I love your ass." Billy ran a hand over Shadow's smooth cheeks. He leaned down and spit on Shadow's hole. He rubbed his finger over Shadow's hole. "Fucking beautiful hole."

Billy took the small bottle of lube that was strategically placed under the blanket. He poured lube down Shadow's crack. Billy pushed the lube into Shadow with one finger. He thrust his finger in, then added a second, and eventually a third, until he was easily sliding in and out.

Billy stepped up behind Shadow. He tapped his cock on Shadow's ass. "Are you ready for this?"

"Yes," Shadow growled.

Billy lined up his dick with Shadow's hole. He rubbed his cock up and down Shadow's glistening crack. With a hand on Shadow's back, he eased in. Pressed against Shadow's ass, Billy ran a hand over the small of Shadow's back, then gave his ass a hard smack.

Shadow moaned at the feel of Billy's cock in him. "Fuck me, Billy. Fuck me with that big dick."

Grunting, Billy slowly pulled half the way out, then slammed hard back into Shadow. He grabbed Shadow by the hips. This time, when he pulled out and thrust back in, he pulled Shadow hard against him. Shadow's body bounced off, but Billy was pulling him back onto his dick.

"Yeah, Billy, do it," Shadow moaned. Reaching under himself, Shadow stroked his cock. "Pound my ass."

Billy pulled out of Shadow. He ordered Shadow, "On your back." Shadow wordlessly flipped onto his back. Billy took his legs and rested them on his shoulders. He pushed into Shadow. Tossing his head back, he drew out his words, "Fuuuuuccccccck yeah."

Shadow returned to stroking his cock. He looked up into Billy's face. Billy was pumping relentlessly into him. He felt every inch of Billy's cock filling him and rubbing that special spot in him. He could feel his balls churning with the temptation of release.

Billy's face contorted into a snarl. Shadow had seen this face before. This was his video orgasm face. Billy's thrusts became quicker, more urgent. Shadow's eyes rolled back in his head. White cream exploded from his cock, smothering his stomach and chest.

Billy let out a snarl. He pulled his cock from Shadow and began stroking furiously. "Fuck! I'm cumming!" Billy shouted as his seed erupted from his cock and splattered all over Shadow. With the last few pulses of his orgasm, he fell on top of Shadow. "I needed that," he said before kissing Shadow.

Shadow put his arms around Billy. He let himself believe the fantasy that Billy and he were together and that what they had done was only for them for just a minute. He ran his hand along Billy's spine, wishing he could still feel Billy's cock in him. He didn't want to let go when Billy pulled away.

Standing over Shadow, the performer mask gone and the impish boyish grin splayed across his face, Billy said, "That was fantastic! I hope they love it!"

"They will." Shadow sat up. The evidence of their tryst slowly ran down his body. "We should get cleaned up before everyone gets back here."

Billy pulled Shadow up to his feet. "You promise I'll see you again?"

"I promise," Shadow lied.

BASED ON REAL EVENTS

"**W**AS THAT A lie?" Jordan asked quietly when Shadow finished his story.

It took a moment for Shadow to answer. "My original plan was for Billy to leave. I was going to sneak away and pay him a visit and never leave." Shadow paused. "It was when Billy had to change who he was in order to fuck me that I realized that no matter what I did, Billy and I wouldn't be any more than friends."

"That must have hurt." Jordan felt sorry for Shadow. He knew that pain, the pain of being just a friend to someone you had feelings for.

Shadow let out a humorless laugh. "It did, but it also gave me hope. Keith and Kevin never came back. Mario wasn't filming much since he had gotten serious with Chris. I figured with Billy gone, that Brett would finally put me first."

"He didn't, did he?" Jordan asked.

Shadow sighed. "No, if anything, it made him more determined. He kept trying to find people to film with, to replace everyone. Joe eventually pulled the plug on it all. He was tired of losing money. Brett went back to webcamming. He tried doing fan content, but the only person he could get to film with him was me. Plus, the videos were filmed and edited horribly."

"What happened to the video you shot with Billy?" Jordan asked, needing to know as much for Billy as for himself.

Jordan heard Shadow shuffle in his seat before he answered. "I gathered the cameras after and hid them in my car. A few days later, Billy got up in the middle of the night and put all his stuff in my car. Later that day, I drove him to the airport and said goodbye. I stopped off at my family's house on the way back and left the cameras there."

"Have you ever watched the videos?" Jordan asked, leaning toward the screen.

There was a long pause before Shadow answered. "No. I knew it would hurt too much to see myself living a fantasy."

"Where is the footage now?" Jordan asked, pointedly.

Shadow's voice went distant. "I uploaded it all to an external drive. It's in a box somewhere around here."

"Will you ever let Billy watch it?" Jordan leaned back against the couch.

Shadow's voice was firm when he answered, "No. I don't want anyone to ever see it."

"What happened after Billy left? Between you and Brett?" Jordan asked, feeling a bit of relief.

Shadow's husband spoke up. "It's okay. Tell him."

"Brett and I grew distant," Shadow explained. "He was only interested in filming. Mario stopped filming completely by then. Mario sat me down one day and asked me what I was doing."

Intrigued, Jordan asked, "What were you doing?"

"Lying to myself," Shadow answered. "I loved Brett, but I wasn't in love with Brett. I know he loved me, too, but he loved his dream more. That hurt more than Billy only seeing me as a friend."

Jordan felt bad about the next question, but he needed to know the answer. "Do you think Billy ever loved you?"

"Billy loved me, but only as a friend. Nothing more. Nothing less. That hurt," Shadow answered.

Jordan glanced at his tablet. One of Billy's questions screamed at him. "Why couldn't Billy contact any of you after he left?"

"I blocked Billy's number on everyone's phone after he left." Shadow snorted. "Mario did it because I asked. Joe and Brett were always handing me their phones to fix something they did on them. It was selfish on my part, but I knew if Billy spoke to any of us, he'd come back. After making that video, seeing him would have been too painful."

Jordan nodded. "When did you decide to leave?"

"It took almost a year before I got the nerve to leave," Shadow said softly. "Brett was out looking for work, and Joe was at a doctor's appointment. I was alone, and I was done with it all. I was done being Shadow. I packed what I wanted to keep, left a note, and sent Mario a text letting him know that I was leaving. Then headed back to my family's house."

Jordan chewed his lip. "Did they try to call you? Text you?"

"Brett did." Sadness crept into Shadow's voice. "Right before I came up here, I changed my number."

Jordan pondered his next question before asking it. "Why did you go there?"

"When I told my parents I left Brett, they were happy but had all these plans for me that I didn't want. We ended up fighting over my future. I got mad and told them I was heading out west and I'd call them when I decided what to do with my future." Happiness flowed into Shadow's voice. "I came here because it was the last place I remembered being happy."

Shadow's husband added, "He didn't expect me to be here when he came."

"It was a welcomed surprise. I thought he left for school." Shadow's voice was full of joy. "I didn't know how to contact him because his number was disconnected."

Jordan instantly regretted his next question as soon as he asked it. "So you didn't know about his injury until you got there?"

"No, I didn't." Shadow paused. "How did you know he has an injury?"

Before Jordan could answer, Shadow's husband spoke up. "I told him."

"When?!" Shadow asked, panicked.

Jordan blurted out, "I made him turn his camera off, I swear!"

"You had the camera on! He saw you?!" Shadow's voice was almost shrill.

Shadow's husband kept his voice calm. "I thought I was leaving him a voicemail."

"That's not how video calling works!" Shadow scolded.

Jordan quickly jumped in. "I told him that. I promise you, I didn't record him on camera, and I refused to take his phone number."

"You tried to give him your number?!" Shadow shouted. Then he paused when Jordan's words hit him. "Wait. You recorded him?"

Jordan swallowed hard. "He wanted to tell me about you, things he didn't think you'd share."

"Like what!?" Shadow shouted through the speakers.

Shadow's husband's voice was soft and loving when he answered. "That you saved my life."

"I didn't save your life," Shadow responded, the heat in his voice gone. "You saved mine."

Jordan quietly asked, "How did you save each other?"

"You are good." Shadow laughed. "One day we're going to be really good friends."

Shadow's husband began, "After my injury, I sort of gave up on life and love. I was broken. I couldn't do my wood carving anymore. I had a hard time moving around, and my hand was practically useless. My dad wanted to move to a warmer climate, but I didn't want to leave."

"Why?" Jordan asked.

Shadow's husband's voice was full of affection. "This is where I met Shadow. Where we first kissed. Where I fell in love with him. I know I cut myself off from him with my injury, but I knew he'd be back

one day. My father wasn't going to leave without me, not the way I was. I couldn't keep him here. I had to do something."

"What did you do?" Shadow asked before Jordan could.

Chris's voice was full of emotion when he answered. "Nerve tests. Spinal injections. Physical therapy. I took medicine that made me sick as a dog and some that made me as high as a kite. I endured painful electro stimulus. Eventually, I got most of my mobility back in my hand. It took about six months before I was off the cane."

"You did that in the hopes of seeing Shadow again?" Jordan asked, putting his hand over his heart.

Chris answered, "Yes. Once my father was sure I could take care of myself, he moved south. I was good for a while. Then I had my first episode. A bad one."

"You never told me," Shadow said, his voice cracking with sorrow. "How bad was it?"

His husband sighed. "Bad. I felt strange that morning when I got up. My head was all jumbled. I was burning up. I couldn't hold anything in my hand. I could barely walk. My brain wasn't scrambled. It was fried. I couldn't think. I was about to pull my phone out to call my doctor, but my hand wouldn't move."

"You don't have to," Shadow said softly.

Shadow's husband continued, his voice trembling when he spoke. "My legs gave out on me, and I collapsed onto the floor. I tried to move. I remember focusing all my energy just to move my finger and it wouldn't move. I was on that floor for almost

four hours, unable to talk or move. I was trapped in my head."

"Oh, baby," Shadow said. Jordan imagined Shadow embracing his husband.

Choked up, Chris continued on, "The only thing I could do was cry and think. I cried because all the work I had done to walk was gone. I cried because I thought I was going to die there on the floor, not having told my dad I loved him one last time or ever seeing Shadow again."

"You don't have to continue," Jordan cut in, getting choked up.

Ignoring Jordan, Shadow's husband continued, "My phone kept going off. I knew it was my dad trying to get a hold of me. I wanted to reach into my pocket to answer him, but no matter how hard I tried, my body wouldn't obey me."

He took a deep breath and let it out. "He got worried and called my doctor and got emergency services out to me. They had to break down the door. They carried me out and took me to the emergency room, where I stayed paralyzed for another four hours."

"How did you recover?" Jordan asked, sitting on the edge of the sofa.

Shadow's husband sighed. "My brain started unscrambling. First, I was able to stutter a few words out. Gradually, I started being able to move my fingers, then my arms. Eventually, I got feeling in my legs. I could walk, but I was unsteady on my legs. I cried myself to sleep in that hospital bed."

"Oh, baby." By the sound of Shadow's voice, he was near tears.

Shadow's husband continued, "When I woke up, my dad was there. He took me home and stayed with me for a few weeks. He tried to convince me to leave with him, but I couldn't leave. We came up with a check-in system in case I had another bad spell."

"You stayed," Shadow said, voice choked up, "for me?"

Shadow's husband answered with love in his voice, "Of course. I knew in my heart you'd come back to me."

"You did not, you big liar," Shadow laughed through his sobs.

Jordan smiled. He hated to interrupt, but he didn't want to continue intruding on this private moment. "How about we pick this up later?"

"Thanks. I'd like to show my husband how much I love him," Shadow answered.

16

YOU WERE WRONG, I WAS RIGHT

SHADOW HELD CHRIS tightly. Tears trickled down his cheeks. "I'm sorry I wasn't here for you then."

Chris returned the embrace, his voice etched with pain. "I didn't want you to see me like that. You see how the people in town look at me."

"Like you're fragile. Like you're about to fall apart at any moment." Shadow buried his face in Chris's chest. "I hate that."

Chris stroked Shadow's hair. "You always looked at me with love, worried you'll lose me."

"To be fair, I did sort of lose you once before," Shadow chastised playfully.

Chris teased back, "Correction, you took your time coming back to me."

"Even when I was here, I still didn't come back to you fully. It took a while. Remember?" Shadow felt the shame in the truth of his words. Remembering the day he knew he had to stay because he couldn't risk losing Chris again. "I was such a fool."

"Thanks for letting me sleep in, baby." Chris came up behind Shadow and put his arms around him. *"I needed it after last night."*

Shadow pulled away. "What are you doing?"

"Giving you a hug," Chris answered, taken aback. *"What's wrong?"*

Shadow cut his eyes at him. "Don't make last night more than what it was. Sex."

"It was more than sex, and you know it." Chris reached with his good hand to take Shadow's, but Shadow evaded his touch. *"Why are you fighting this?"*

Shadow snapped. "I'm not fighting anything. I need a friend right now, not a lover."

"Okay." Chris turned away, hurt. Walking away, he started clenching and unclenching his left hand. His arm started to shake.

Shadow watched Chris with a guilty scowl. The anger quickly turned to panic when he saw Chris's left leg give out. Rushing to catch him, Shadow cried out, "Chris!" He fell into Shadow's arms. "Are you okay?"

"Yeah." Chris let Shadow move him to a kitchen chair.

Concerned, Shadow kneeled down to look Chris in the eye. "I'm going to make you something to eat. Where are your meds?"

"I don't want you to fuss over me, and I don't want to take any meds," Chris answered, eyes glassy and shaking his head.

Shadow took Chris's hands in his. "You said if I stayed, you'd follow the doctor's orders. That means taking your medicine."

"I flushed them last night after you slipped them into my food." Chris lowered his head guiltily.

Shadow lifted Chris's chin up so he was looking him in the eyes. "While I make you something to eat, you call the doctor and get them refilled. Then I want you to schedule your physical therapy."

"Fine." Chris grinned. "Can I have French toast?"

Shadow stood up. "Okay, let me get you some orange juice."

Shadow surreptitiously listened to Chris on the phone while he cooked. He smirked. By the sound of Chris's quiet and meek tone, whoever it was on the other end of the line was obviously chastising him for not calling sooner. That little joy quickly turned to guilt, because he felt he could have come back sooner.

His self-pity was interrupted by Chris's remorseful voice. "She wants to speak to you."

"What?" Shadow asked, flipping the French toast in the pan before turning around to see Chris holding out his phone. Taking the phone and putting it to his ear, Shadow hesitantly spoke into the phone, "Hello, this is Shadow."

A stern older woman's voice answered, "This is Nurse Drew. Is the man that is currently living with Chris and is taking on the responsibility of ensuring his care for at least the next six months?"

"Six months?" Shadow barely squeaked out.

Nurse Drew came back curtly. "Yes, when he restarts the medicine, he'll not be allowed to be alone for long periods

of time or drive for three months. Winter is coming and he'll need someone to winterize his place."

"Winter is only three months." Shadow turned back to the stove and flipped the French toast.

Nurse Drew made a sound of annoyance. "You must not be local, otherwise you'd know how long the snow lasts here. Snow starts in November and can last until April. If you're not going to stick around, I won't refill his prescriptions. I need to know someone is going to stick around to watch him, get him to his appointments, and take care of him."

"I'll be here for as long as it takes for him," Shadow responded sternly. He flipped the last piece of French toast onto a plate. Carrying it over to Chris, he said, "Go ahead and refill his prescriptions, schedule all his rehabilitation appointments, and write down any instructions we need." Shadow grabbed the maple syrup off the counter. He held it just out of reach from Chris's outstretched hand. "He's supposed to lose weight, isn't he?"

Nurse Drew answered, "Yes and no. If he can strengthen his muscles just a little bit he wouldn't have his episodes so often."

"Episodes?" Shadow gave a scowling Chris the syrup. Turning back to look out the window, he said, "You mean like when he shakes and falls?"

Chris spoke up with a little bite in his voice. "I don't have episodes."

"He's lying," Nurse Drew responded over the phone. "That's why I need to know someone will be there for him. The medicine is supposed to help stabilize his nerves, but we'll have to adjust his dosage and mix to get it right so he can function normally."

Shadow turned around to see Chris merrily eating. Maple syrup dripped down his chin. "There are going to be a lot of changes around here."

"Changes?" Chris asked around a mouth full of food.

Shadow ignored Chris's question. "Can I stop by and meet with you sometime today?"

"Absolutely. Come at one. I'll make time for you." There was a smile in Nurse Drew's voice.

"I'll see you at one, thank you." Shadow hung the phone up.

Looking at Shadow curiously, Chris repeated, "Changes?"

"Yes. I'm getting rid of all the junk food in this house." Shadow crossed his arms. "For the next six months, we're eating healthy in this house." He watched the biggest smile stretch across Chris's face. "Why are you smiling?"

Smugly Chris said, "You said you'll be here for six months." Chris popped a piece of French toast in his mouth. Chewing it slowly, he watched Shadow with amusement. "I'll have you fall in love with me in a month."

"I'll have you hating me in a month and screaming not to touch you," Shadow shot back.

Shadow looked deep into Chris's eyes. "You were wrong, and I was right."

"About?" Chis asked curiously.

Shadow's body shook with a silent laugh. "The day after our first night together, you said you'd have me fall in love with you in a month." Shadow pulled

Chris closer. "I was already in love with you. I didn't want to admit it."

"I knew that. I just wanted to give you time to realize it," Chris teased. "What were you right about?"

Shadow rubbed his nose against Chris's. "That you'd be hating me and screaming not to touch you."

"I didn't hate you. I hated that you kept making me do those exercises and that you kept throwing out my snack stashes." Chris pecked Shadow on the lips. "I never hated you touching me."

BILLY AND JORDAN'S FIRST TIME

SITTING ON THE couch in Lexi's living room. Jordan tried not to look scared or guilty. The text message he got from Lexi summoning him to her place came shortly after ending the interview with Shadow and his husband. He knew he was in trouble. He was supposed to be with Billy.

Jordan pulled out his phone and began scrolling through his pictures. *I wish I was with him right now,* Jordan thought, smiling at the puppy-dog-eyed picture Billy had sent him from the airport. He brushed his finger over the picture. *That first time we made love, I was so scared. He made me feel so special.*

Exhausted and feeling the desperate need for a shower, Jordan opened the door of the cheap motel. A blast of stuffy, hot air assaulted him. He took an unusually quiet

Billy by the hand and pulled him along into the room with 1980s decor. They had spent eight hours at the police station being grilled about the Country Boyz murders.

Jordan turned the wall unit on full blast before falling back onto the bed. He was grateful Lexi Luscious had given him her phone number before they left. Had her attorneys not gotten involved, they'd probably be sitting in a jail cell being accused of murder.

He watched Billy drop their bag on the floor, then head to the bathroom. He heard the shower turn on. A few moments later, Billy came out naked. Wordlessly, he walked to the bed, took Jordan by the hand, and pulled him from the bed. He undid Jordan's pants, then started tugging on Jordan's shirt.

Confused, Jordan asked softly, "Billy, what are you doing?"

"Getting you undressed so we can take a shower," Billy answered, looking Jordan in the eyes. His face brightened with a smile. "We're dating now, remember?"

Jordan lifted his arms up to let Billy pull off his shirt. "About that. I know you only said that because of what happened. I'm not going to hold you to that."

"Really? I am." Billy pushed down Jordan's pants and underwear. "Jordan, you are the kindest, sweetest person I know. You let me into your apartment and life. I didn't even realize we were dating until other people pointed it out." Billy's face brightened. "The thought of dating you, you, Jordan, made me so happy, and then I was so nervous about talking to you about being my boyfriend. Don't you understand? You're a fantastic guy and I'm just Billy."

Jordan shook his head, trying to make sense of Billy's words. "What are you talking about? Why would you be

nervous? You're Billy, the porn star. You're beautiful. I'm just me, the work-from-home-at-a-dead-end-customer-service-job struggling writer."

"You say you're only Jordan, but to me, you're the man I can't stop thinking about. When we're apart, I can't wait to be together again, and I am happiest when I snuggle with you in bed." Billy looked around the room. "I know this isn't really a romantic place to share our first kiss, but I have to kiss you."

Flustered, Jordan stumbled over his words. "Billy, wow, um, I'm the same way." Jordan closed his eyes and gathered his thoughts. He opened them to see a grinning Billy. "You have turned my world upside down. You've given me encouragement and opportunities that I can't thank you enough for. You invaded my life and my bed, and I can't imagine either without you."

"Does that mean what I think it means?" Billy asked, putting his hands on Jordan's hips.

Putting his arms around Billy's neck, Jordan said, "That means kiss me, you fool."

Even with their naked bodies pressed close and Billy's lips pressed to his, Jordan still couldn't believe it was happening. This is a dream. A delusion. I'm still lying in bed. This isn't real. *Billy's hardness pressed into his leg.* Nope. That's a penis. A very hard and very long penis. This is really happening.

Jordan relaxed when he felt Billy's hands move around to hold him. Stop thinking, *he ordered himself.* Be in this moment. Be with Billy.

Billy gave his butt a playful pop before pulling away from the kiss. He was smiling gleefully at Jordan. "Get out of your head, Teddy Bear." He pulled away, taking

Jordan's hand as they broke apart. "Let's shower." Billy wrinkled his nose. "You stink."

"I stink?!" Jordan exclaimed a moment after the words hit him. "You stink."

Billy pulled Jordan into the bathroom. "Then we both better get clean so we can get dirty again."

"There's not enough room for both of us in there," Jordan protested weakly, letting himself be pulled into the tiny tub with Billy.

With their bodies pressed close together, chest to chest, and water cascading over them, Billy said, "When you write about us, make sure you give us a happily ever after."

"That means our story has to have a happy ending." Jordan brushed the wet hair from Billy's face.

Billy grinned impishly. "Oh, I'm going to give you so many happy endings."

"And I'm going to give us a happily ever after." Jordan kissed Billy.

Billy pulled Jordan close. "We better get started."

Kissing him again as the shower rained down on them, Jordan's hands roamed Billy's body. He felt the softness of Billy's skin, the hardness of his muscles. The gentle slope of Billy's back which arched to a perfect bubble butt that Jordan had resisted touching until now.

Billy's touch felt like magic to Jordan. It sent shivers and sparks through him. His touch made Jordan comfortable in his skin. Billy didn't shy away from touching him, like so many others had when they felt his chubby body. Billy's touch was soft, tender, and loving. Jordan couldn't recall any of his partners ever touching him like that.

"Let's get you clean." Taking the washcloth, Billy began soaping up Jordan's chest. "Your heart is racing, like mine." Billy took Jordan's hand and put it on his chest. "See?"

Jordan felt Billy's heart thumping in his chest. "I know why mine is. Why is yours?"

"This is the first time I'm going to have sex with someone who truly loves me back." Billy turned Jordan around and began washing his back. "You're the first person I truly trust with my heart."

Turning around, Jordan took the cloth from Billy and began washing him. "You're the first person who made me truly feel special, made me feel like I matter. You know you're the first person that has seen me without my shirt on in a very long time?"

"I meant what I said back home." Billy ran a hand over Jordan's wet, matted chest hair. "I never want you to hide your body from me."

Jordan spun Billy around into the spray. He smiled at the thought of Billy calling his place home. He ran the cloth over Billy's broad back. Jordan laughed. "I'm naked in a shower with Billy, the porn star. You've seen it all now. I don't think there's any point in trying to hide anything after this."

Billy turned around to let the shower wash away the soap. He shook the water from his hair. He gave Jordan a lustful look. "Yeah, well, in a few minutes, you're going to be making love to Billy, your boyfriend, who happens to be a porn star."

"Billy, you know it's been a while for me," Jordan said nervously.

Billy turned the water off, then grabbed towels. "Don't worry." Billy stepped out of the tub. "It's like riding a dick. You never forget how."

"I didn't forget how," Jordan said, drying himself. He caught Billy grinning at him. Throwing his towel at Billy, Jordan exclaimed, "You jerk!"

Billy caught the towel and started drying Jordan's hair. "We can go as fast or slow as you need." Billy started drying the rest of Jordan's body. "You know, I think your hair is all wild and crazy because you don't get to be."

"I'll show you wild and crazy." Stepping out of the tub, Jordan crushed his mouth to Billy's.

Bodies pressed together, their hands explored, their tongues intertwined. Jordan pushed Billy against the vanity. He moaned into the kiss at the feel of Billy's crotch rubbing against his. Billy pushed off the vanity and they stumbled back into the room. Their bodies tangled when they fell onto the bed with Billy on top.

Billy took Jordan's hands and pinned them to the bed. He pulled back from the kiss. He looked down at Jordan salaciously and quickly pecked Jordan on the lips. Then on each cheek. "You're mine now," he said with a slight growl in his voice. He licked the tip of Jordan's nose.

"Did you just lick me?" Jordan laughed, playfully struggling against Billy's grip.

Billy licked Jordan's nose again. "Yup. I licked you so you're mine now."

"Oh, yeah." Jordan rolled them over so he was on top. "Is that how it works?"

Billy tried to lean up to lick Jordan again. "Yeah, got a problem with that?"

"No, but you might when you find out what I lick." Jordan let go of Billy's arms and sat back on his heels. He took Billy's legs and pressed them to his chest, revealing Billy's smooth hole.

Billy pulled his legs back farther, almost curling himself into a ball. "It's all yours."

"You're damn right it is." Jordan's voice was a mix of playful and dominating.

Jordan pressed his face between Billy's hard, muscled cheeks. He swirled his tongue around the soft skin. Billy groaned and pulled his legs back farther. "Fuck yeah, it's yours. Anytime you want it."

Jordan pressed Billy's thighs farther into him. He began lapping his tongue against Billy's hole, adding in long, slow swipes. He felt Billy's body jolt slightly when he zig-zagged his tongue up and down. Whenever Billy's moans or breath seemed to calm, Jordan switched his technique to send him skyrocketing back up.

After a long teasing lick up Billy's crack, Jordan looked Billy in the eyes. Smugly he said in a deep growly voice, "I licked it, so it's mine."

"Anytime you want it," Billy moaned.

Jordan lowered Billy's legs. His eyes darted down to Billy's hard cock laying there begging for attention. He looked back into Billy's eyes. "That's not the only thing I'm going to lick."

"Lick every part of me," Billy begged. "Make me yours, now and forever."

Jordan licked from the base of Billy's balls to the tip of his cock. He fought the urge to gorge himself. He lifted Billy's cock up to the sky and licked around the crown before

taking Billy into his mouth. Billy's hands started running through his hair. Jordan groaned.

Jordan slipped seven of Billy's ten inches past his lips. He moved slowly along Billy's length. He could feel the soft throb of Billy's cock against his tongue. Billy arched his hips up with a groan. Billy's hands tightened in his hair. Jordan worked Billy's cock faster.

Billy pulled Jordan off his cock and kissed him. "Mind if I reciprocate?"

"How about a tradeoff instead?" Jordan moved up alongside Billy.

Billy pecked Jordan on the lips. "Sounds good to me."

Billy flipped around and Jordan lay on his side, cock facing Billy. Jordan gasped at the feel of Billy's warm mouth around his cock. Billy's hand gripped his ass. He pulled Jordan's hips toward him, fucking his mouth with Jordan's cock. Jordan reveled in the feeling before mirroring Billy's actions.

Enjoying Billy's cock and the feel of Billy enjoying his, Jordan grew a little bold and slipped a finger between Billy's tight, muscled cheeks. He rubbed his finger over Billy's rosebud. Billy whimpered with need. Jordan pushed the finger in. Billy started gently thrusting his hips, fucking Jordan's mouth while fucking himself on Jordan's finger.

Billy pulled off Jordan's cock, shouting a lustful command. "I need you in me now!"

"We don't have any lube," Jordan said, pulling off Billy's cock.

Billy moved off the bed and to the bag he dropped on the floor. "You grabbed my overnight bag from the apartment." Billy reached into one of the side pockets and pulled out a bottle of lube. "Always carry emergency lube."

Jordan laughed as he watched Billy pour the lube onto his fingers and begin to prep himself. "I'll remember that for the future."

"Your turn, Teddy Bear." Billy climbed back onto the bed and began stroking Jordan's hard-on. "I'm going to ride you until the cows come home."

Gazing up into Billy's face, Jordan let out a sigh as Billy lowered himself onto his full length. Taking Billy by the waist, Jordan moaned huskily, "Oh, Billy."

Billy rolled his hips while rising up and down. Jordan's left hand moved up to wander over his chest. His right hand found its way to Billy's cock. Jordan began stroking Billy's hard rod. Pre-cum dribbled out of the tip onto Jordan's belly. Jordan began pumping in time with Billy's movements.

"When we get home," Billy groaned, "I'm going to do so many naughty things to you."

Jordan started thrusting up harder. "Oh, and you don't think I have some dirty things I want to do to you?"

"Tell me," Billy ordered, leaning over to look Jordan in the face.

Jordan put his arms around Billy and rolled them over so he was on top. "I'd rather show you." Jordan kissed him. "Remember, I'm a writer. We show, not tell."

"Show me then," Billy panted. "Fuck, Jordan," Billy crooned, racking his nails down Jordan's back. "How are you doing that?"

Jordan began thrusting faster into Billy. "Doing what?"

"Hitting my spot." Billy dug his fingers into Jordan's back. Breathless, he added, "Every time."

Jordan began pumping faster into Billy. "I don't know." He kissed Billy. "Billy, I'm sorry. It's been a while and I'm not going to last much longer."

"Don't be sorry. You've got me on the edge, too." Billy pulled Jordan down into a kiss.

Jordan began letting out soft whimpers. His hips slammed into Billy. He sucked on Billy's lower lip. His body began to quiver with the intensity building in his balls. He kissed Billy hard and deep as his juices surged up his shaft. He furiously pounded into Billy.

"Billy," Jordan cried out softly. His body went stiff and shook with the intensity of his cock exploding deep inside Billy. "Oh, God! Oh, Billy!" Jordan cried out. He pumped his cock rapidly as what felt like a tsunami was unleashed. He kissed Billy feverishly as the last currents of his orgasm flowed through his body and he collapsed on top of Billy.

Billy ran his hands up and down Jordan's back. Jordan slipped out of Billy and off to the side. He took Billy's cock in his hand and began stroking him. "Your turn."

"Kiss me." Billy pulled Jordan close.

Jordan slipped his tongue into Billy's mouth. He felt Billy's cock swell. Billy began letting out soft moans and began thrusting up into Jordan's hand. Billy held onto Jordan tighter as his body began shaking. His legs kicked out and thumped down on the bed.

"Jordan!" Billy cried out into the kiss as rope after rope shot from his dick and splattered across him and Jordan. Billy jolted with each pump of Jordan's hand. "Jordan," he said between convulsions. "Jordan. Stop. Sensitive."

Jordan gave him one last stroke before letting go and moving his hand to Billy's chest. "We actually did it."

"Yeah, we did," Billy chuckled. "We're going to do it again and again and again." Jordan laid his head on Billy's chest. Randomly, Billy said, "I wonder what happened to Shadow. He was my best friend at the house. I hope he's okay."

Jordan shifted to look at Billy. "I'll find out for you. I promise."

"I know you will." Billy ran a hand through Jordan's hair. "How about we take another shower and go to bed?"

"I'm sorry to keep you waiting." Lexi's voice brought Jordan out of his thoughts. She glided into the room and sat down in one of the overstuffed chairs. She raised an eyebrow at Jordan. "On second thought, no, I'm not sorry to keep you waiting. What are you doing here?"

Jordan looked everywhere but at Lexi when he said, "You texted me to come over immediately."

Lexi was unamused when she spoke. "You know what I mean. You told me you were going with Billy. I found out from Hunter that you changed your flight because you were working on something for me. What are you doing?"

"I wanted a little time to myself. Sort of a staycation," Jordan lied.

Lexi gave Jordan a stern look. "Don't bullshit a bullshitter. You and Billy are inseparable, except when you have work conflicts. He has work, and I made sure you had no projects, so you could help Hunter and

Mark and enjoy their bachelor party." Lexi crossed her arms. "I'll ask you again. What are you doing here?"

"Please, don't be mad," Jordan cringed. "I stayed behind because I got a lead on Shadow."

Lexi closed her eyes, centering herself and choosing her words carefully. "Jordan, I told you to stop looking for Shadow. You're wasting your time, and it brings Billy nothing but pain every time you hit a dead end."

"Not this time." Jordan's body tingled. "I found him. I've been interviewing him over video chat since Billy left." Jordan's eyes began to water. "It's him. It's really him. I found him for Billy."

Lexi sat there, stunned for a moment. "Are you certain? Are you one hundred percent certain?"

"He knew things only Shadow would know." Jordan wiped away a tear. "I've talked to him and his husband."

Lexi sat on the edge of her chair. "I want to see everything you've got so far. Is he okay with sharing his face with the world again?"

"No, and no." Jordan sat a little straighter, ready for a fight. "Shadow agreed to the interview as long as we didn't show his face and that Billy got to see the recordings first."

Lexi chewed her lower lip. "Billy should be the first to see it all. It's only right." She sat back in her chair. "How are you going to do this? Written story like always?"

"No." Jordan shook his head. "I want to do it like a video interview. I'll cut some things out to get it down, but I'm on camera and I think it would make a great video piece along with a written story."

Lexi did a double take. "You don't like being on camera."

"Things change." Jordan shrugged. "Speaking to Shadow and his husband has inspired me to make quite a few changes."

Lexi crossed her legs. "Oh, do tell."

"No spoilers," Jordan teased. "How was your meeting with Paris?"

Lexi thought for a moment. "Boring at first, then he wowed me. I think he's going to make a great addition to the team. Oh, and that sexy boyfriend cook of his? Yummy. He's going to have him do a cooking show pilot for us. I'll send you the link when he does. I want your opinion."

"Is that the attack twink Billy told me about?" Jordan asked.

Lexi smirked, "Probably. He seems like a feisty one."

"I hate to cut this short, but I have an appointment I need to get to." Jordan stood.

Lexi stood. "Jordan, next time I give you an order, you better listen." She went over and hugged him. "Unless your gut tells you differently."

"Better to ask forgiveness than permission, right?" Jordan joked, hugging her back. "I really have to go. There's something important I have to get."

Lexi looked at him questioningly. "Oh?"

"No spoilers," Jordan said with a wink.

18

CHRIS'S WOOD

SHADOW AIMLESSLY WALKED up and down the front porch, pulling random dead leaves off the plants. Chris was in the barn-turned-workshop covering himself in wood shavings as he worked on one of his projects. He didn't like that Chris was alone handling complicated sharp tools, but he was happy Chris had returned to his art.

It was a week after they shared their first night together that Shadow learned about Chris's passion for carving wood. Chris was still getting used to being back on his meds. Some days were good, and they could go for short walks together in the woods and do his exercises. Some days were okay, and he could do some of his exercises. Most days were bad, and he had to tend to Chris.

Chris would be good for a little while after he woke up. His mind would be a little foggy. Shadow still watched him covertly. He saw the slight trembles in Chris's hand. How he would shake it and flex his fingers before trying to pick something up with it. He saw Chris pause before taking steps as if he had to will his leg to move.

Then the medicine would hit. Chris would get disoriented. He'd be sitting, staring out into nothingness. He'd look at Shadow as if he didn't know who he was. Sometimes he'd fidget and shake as his nerves went into overload and he'd be overwhelmed by thoughts. Those days, Shadow would take him in his arms and lay down with him until it passed.

He was lying with Chris on the bed, stroking his hair. It was a particularly bad morning for Chris. He needed to lay down and rest from his nerves going haywire. Chris had barely closed his eyes before he had passed out from exhaustion. The only reason Shadow had left him sleeping in the bed was because of someone knocking on the door.

Shadow opened the front door to see a handsome Black man a few years older than him, dressed in jeans and an athletic shirt that showcased his tight, toned body cheerily grinning at him. When he saw Shadow, confusion crossed his face. "Who are you?"

"I'm Shadow. Who are you?" Shadow responded defensively.

The stranger looked him up and down. "I'm Scott. I came to check up on Chris. Is he here?"

"He's sleeping," Shadow said, a little more defensively than he intended. "I'll tell him you stopped by."

Scott gave Shadow a lopsided smirk. "No need to be jealous, man. Chris and I broke up a long time ago. I'm just here to check up on him, see if he needs any help winterizing the house, and bring him a truckload of wood." He stepped aside so Shadow could see his truck full of wood. "I brought a few big pieces in case Chris decides he wants to try woodcarving again."

"Woodcarving? He does woodcarving?" Shadow glanced back over his shoulder to the room where Chris was sleeping.

Scott brought his attention back when answered. "Yeah, some pretty nice pieces. I got him to start selling them in the local stores. The big pieces don't sell as quickly, but the tourists love his smaller pieces."

"Wait," Shadow said, needing to clarify Scott's earlier statement. "Did you say you and Chris dated? When?"

Scott flashed a cocky grin. "He didn't tell you about me?" Shadow shook his head. "Figures. I was new in town. Hit him up online. We hit it off and dated for three months. I ended it because he was pining away for some dude named—"

"Me," Shadow finished.

Scott shifted uncomfortably. "Yeah, um, how about I go unload this wood and get going? You can give Chris my love."

"Scott, Chris isn't going to be able to winterize the house, and I don't know what to do. Could you," Shadow fidgeting nervously, "help me get the house ready?"

Scott nodded, "Sure."

"Scott," Shadow said before he could turn away, "you wouldn't know where I can see some of Chris's work, would you?"

Scott's face brightened. "You haven't been in the barn yet." He waved Shadow to follow him. "Let me show you Chris's workshop."

"Okay." Shadow glanced back at the room before following behind. "I haven't been in the barn since I got here. Actually, I don't think I ever have."

Scott tugged open the creaking door. "I don't think he's been in here since his injury." Scott flipped the lights on. "It might be a little dustier than normal."

The overhead lights flickered into life, casting a dull yellow glow on several work tables loaded with tools and machines that Shadow had no clue how to use. Woodchips, sawdust, and dust covered everything. On a table in the corner, sat a single item covered in a white sheet.

"I don't see any of his pieces," Shadow said, glancing around.

Scott went straight to the table in the corner. "There's one piece he'll never part with." He motioned Shadow over. "Go ahead, look at it."

"What are you two doing in here?!" Chris shouted from the door.

Turning to look at him, Shadow explained, "Scott told me about your woodcarving and was going to show me one of your pieces."

"He has no right to show you that one." Swaying, Chris made his way to the table.

Holding his hands up in supplication, Scott apologized. "I'm sorry. I overstepped."

"Scott, I think you should go," Chris snapped. "Now."

Scott nodded. "I'll unload the wood and be off." To Shadow, he said, "Chris has my number. Call me."

"Call him?" Chris accused. "So, are you two fucking now?"

Shadow crossed his arms. "If we were, what business is it of yours? I told you that we're not an item."

"As you like to remind me every single time I try to get close to you." Chris put a hand on the table to steady himself. "What happened to you? Why won't you tell me what you were doing these past three years?"

Shadow tensed. His voice quivered with anger. He directed it at Chris, but it was all at himself. "Do you really want to know? I'll tell you." Chris stood there silently, waiting for him to continue. "I was filming porn. I escorted. I was dating a guy, and we filmed ourselves having sex with each other and other men for his website. I slept with men for money and fun. That's what happened to me."

"That's what you did. What happened to you?" Chris narrowed his eyes at him. "What happened to you? What made you leave?"

Shadow's eyes began to sting with tears. "I left because he cared more about his failing porn site than he did about me, okay? He loved me, but he was never going to put me first. Then there was…" Shadow looked away from Chris. "Then there was the fact I didn't have you anymore." Tears trickled down Shadow's cheeks. "Why am I not good enough for the men I love?"

"You've always been good enough for me." Chris wiped a tear from his cheek. "You'll always be my number one."

Shadow looked at him accusingly. "Then why did you cut me off? Why didn't you call me and tell me what happened?"

"I know that was selfish of me." Chris took one of Shadow's hands and pulled it away from his chest. "I was

in a dark place then. I wanted to call you so many times, but I knew if I did, you'd drop everything to come see me." Chris raised Shadow's hand to his mouth and kissed it. "I was a shell of the person I was when you knew me. I didn't start feeling like myself again until I saw you on the front porch. You don't know how happy that made me."

Shadow reluctantly admitted, "I do. It's as happy as I was to see you." Shadow shook his head. "I keep telling you, I can't give you what you want. I'm broken, and you can't fix me."

"Open your eyes. I'm broken, too," Chris said imploringly. "I don't want to fix you. I just want to love you and be broken with you."

Shadow looked at him sympathetically. "You're not broken. You're injured. There's a difference."

"I'm not talking about my injury." Chris let go of his hand. "It's what the injury did to me emotionally and mentally." He looked over at the sheet-covered carving. "This piece means the world to me. It's of the moment that I held onto to get me through my dark times." He looked back at Shadow. "I'd like to show it to you."

A slight smile crept across Shadow's face. "I'd be honored."

"I hope you like it." Chris pulled the sheet off.

Shadow's eyes grew wide. "Is that?"

"Us," Chis answered. "Our first kiss out in the snow."

Shadow ran a hand over the intricately carved piece of wood. There was no mistaking the two boys holding each other and kissing. Chris had every detail about that moment perfectly etched into the wood. "It's amazing."

"Thank you." There was a pain in Chris's voice. "Too bad I can't carve like that anymore."

Shadow turned back to Chris. "You will. We're going to get those meds right. We're going to do your exercises and rehabilitation and we're going to get you back to yourself."

"We'll get you back to yourself, too. Maybe even love again." Chris said hopefully.

Shadow sighed. He wiped away a stray tear. "We'll be kissing out in the freezing snow again before that happens."

Seeing Chris come out of the barn covered in sawdust broke Shadow's reverie. He smiled to himself, stepped off the porch, and met his confused husband halfway. Putting his arms around Chris, Shadow gave him a deep, passionate kiss.

"What was that for?" Chris asked.

Shadow smiled lovingly back at him. "For never giving up on me."

"You never gave up on me." Chris smiled back.

Taking Chris's hand, they walked back to the house. "Let's go get cleaned up. I want to make that video for Billy, and I want you in it."

JORDAN GETS REAL

"**O**KAY, BOYS, THIS is the last time I'm changing flight itineraries." Lexi's voice came over the speaker of Jordan's phone. "Jordan, you'll stay here and finish your Shadow interviews. I want them done before you see Billy."

Cameron quickly protested. "I wanted him to come here and look at what I got."

"Want in one hand and shit in the other and see which one fills up first," Lexi scolded before letting out a groan of dismay. "I can't believe I said that."

Jordan started laughing. "You've been hanging around Billy too much."

"Fine," Cameron huffed. "Jordan, I do need to get with you later about Alex. He wants to apologize to you. He was hoping to do it in person."

Jordan looked over at his waiting computer. "These interviews with Shadow are too important. Not just for Billy, but me, too."

"Oh?" Lexi asked.

Cameron chimed in, "You sound different. Are you okay?"

"Yeah, talking to Shadow and his husband has really been eye-opening," Jordan answered.

Cameron sighed. "I know what you mean. It's the same with Alex and Owen."

"Boys, you two can have girl talk later. We need to finish this conference call," Lexi broke in. "I have a hotel room for Alex and Owen. You two can go there after your planes land and get ready for the wedding."

Jordan stiffened. "Alex is coming to the wedding? After everything he's done to everyone?"

"Hunter wants him at the wedding. This is his and Mark's wedding, not anyone else's," Lexi said firmly.

Cameron then added, "He has changed; he wants to apologize and make amends with everyone he's wronged."

"Are you going to make amends with Carlos?" Lexi asked pointedly.

Jordan added, "Carlos was in the wrong, but you did antagonize him, Cameron."

"I know," Cameron huffed. "I have to tell him what's going on with Alex and Owen when I do. I think we should wait until after the wedding for me to tell him."

They were silent, listening to the sound of Lexi tapping her nails on her desk. "Good idea. I know you boys are in the wedding, but I want you to show up last minute and you are to keep your distance from your men, especially you, Jordan. You know you can't keep anything from Billy. We'll gather everyone after for a big formal announcement."

"We may need an extra room for me if things don't go well with Billy." Jordan wrapped his arms around himself. "This could make or break us."

Cameron asked worriedly, "What aren't you telling us?"

"Shadow isn't ready to see Billy yet." Jordan then reluctantly added, "I don't think he'll ever be, and I can't tell Billy where he is."

Sympathetically, Lexi said, "At least he'll know Shadow is safe. He might be upset for a little while, but he'll come around. If need be, you can bunk with Ryan in my two-bedroom suite. That is, if Ryan doesn't find himself in someone else's bed."

"I'll be there for you, man," Cameron added. "I'll get Carlos to talk to him if need be."

Jordan felt a little more at ease. "Thank you. Both of you."

"Anytime," Lexi said with a smile in her voice. "I hate to cut this short, but I have another meeting to get to. Keep me posted on your projects, and when Paris sends me his pilot video, I'll forward it to you to get your opinions. Are we good boys?"

Cameron spoke first. "Yes, Aunt Lexi."

"Yes," Jordan said after a moment of hesitation.

"Jordan, don't worry. Billy loves you. He might get upset for a while, but he'll come around. Now, I really have to go. Bye, boys. Love you," Lexi said right before ending the call.

Jordan picked his phone up. He checked the time; he knew Billy would be filming. That meant his phone would be off or on silent. He wouldn't get to talk to

Billy, but he'd hear his voice on the voicemail. That's what Jordan needed right now, to hear Billy's voice.

Jordan pressed Billy's number. Straight to voicemail, as he hoped. He smiled when he heard Billy's recorded voice. "This is Billy. Leave me a message and your contact information. I'll get back to you as soon as I can."

"Billy, it's Jordan. I know you're filming. I wanted to call and tell you that I miss you and that I love you. I'll see you soon." Jordan ended the call before he started babbling on.

Jordan's phone dinged with the notification of an email. Jordan woke up his computer. The email was from Shadow. There was a brief message and a link.

Jordan,

Here's the video for Billy. I hope it gives him some closure and that he shares it with you one day.

Shadow

Jordan clicked the link, and the video began downloading. His writer's curiosity tingled. He wanted to watch the video as soon as it was downloaded but couldn't. This video was for Billy. If Billy chose to share it with him after, then he'd get to see it.

Jordan hit reply.

Thank you so much for doing this. I promise I won't watch it unless Billy says I can.

Jordan.

Jordan looked at the picture of Billy on his phone. He was lost in his mind, overthinking every possible scenario when his video conferencing program came to life with an incoming call. For a moment, he was

scared it was Billy and was oddly relieved when he saw it was Shadow's name on the screen.

Jordan clicked accept and said, "Shadow, thank you so much for that video for Billy."

"You're welcome. It gave me closure. I hope it does the same for him." Shadow paused, then asked, concerned, "Are you okay? You look a little upset."

Jordan shrugged. "I'm missing Billy, and I'm worried about what's going to happen to us after he finds out I've been talking to you."

"Do you want to talk about it?" Shadow asked. "I have time. My husband's in his workshop playing with his wood."

Jordan blurted out, "Excuse me?"

"He carves wooden sculptures," Shadow laughed. "He got inspired and had to work on it."

Jordan chuckled. "I can relate."

"So let's talk." Shadow's voice was warm and friendly. "I'd like to get to know you."

Jordan smiled. "Do you mind if I record this? It'll be off the record, but I might want to show Billy one day."

"Be my guest. This conversation is all about you," Shadow answered.

Jordan clicked the record button. "Okay, we're recording."

"Great," Shadow said merrily. "What do you famous people say? Dish, bitch?"

Jordan shook his head. "I'm not famous. I'm only a writer. I'm famous adjacent."

"Are you not the creator and writer of the popular web series, *Diva Porn Star?* Don't you write for several blogs and studios now?" Shadow asked.

Jordan rolled his eyes. "Yes, but I'm the guy behind the scenes. I write words. People don't know who I am."

"I did," Shadow responded.

Jordan argued, "That's only because of Billy. No one would know who I was if it wasn't for Billy."

"Billy gave you the opportunity. You proved yourself," Shadow countered. "Why is that so hard for you to accept?"

Jordan fell back into the couch. "I had big dreams, once upon a time. When my company closed my center down, I took advantage of the relocation and moved to California. I had hopes of making it big as a writer. I didn't realize how hard it was going to be. It took so long for me to make friends. Real friends, that is."

Jordan sighed. "I wasn't fashionable enough, skinny enough, or rich enough. The few friends I did make were all trying to be like the 'in' crowd. Me? I just wanted to write and find love. Ironically, they all did find love and settled down. Then my company told us we could work from home or find other work."

"So you were the single guy stuck at home," Shadow commented. "Did it give you more time to write?"

Jordan shook his head. "No. I started dating this guy. He…" Jordan swallowed hard. "He wasn't a very nice guy."

"He didn't hit you? Did he?" Shadow asked, concern evident in his voice.

Jordan smiled weakly at the screen. "No, but you don't need to hit someone to hurt them." Jordan took

a deep breath. "I've always struggled with body image. I was always bigger, trying to get smaller. I never liked to take my shirt off in front of anyone. This guy was so handsome and sexy and he wanted to date me."

"What happened?" Shadow asked softly.

Jordan paused to gather his words. "He was nice, at first. Then the playful jabs started happening. Silly, stupid things that didn't really hurt, but got under my skin. He'd call me his little piggy. He'd grab my chest and say things like, 'You're almost a D cup.' Of course, I'd just laugh it off."

Jordan held himself tightly. "I laughed it off because hey, I had a boyfriend and I could do couple-things with my friends, and he never said these things in front of my friends or in public." Jordan closed his eyes. "Then things got worse."

Jordan opened his eyes. "We'd be out to eat, and he'd order for us. Steak for him, and salad with no dressing for his piggy date. He started calling me Shamu in front of my friends. If I was eating something, he'd ask me if I really needed to be eating that much or he'd tell me to exercise, then if I did, he'd look at me and say things like, what's the point? If he saw me writing, he'd snatch it from me and read it, then tell me how horrible it was, that I should get a clue and realize I didn't have any talent. I actually stopped writing for a while. It wasn't until Billy came into my life that I started writing again."

"He sounds like a dick," Shadow commented. "Obviously, you broke up with him."

Jordan nodded as tears trickled down his cheeks. "I did, but not before he alienated me from my friends

and amplified my own self-loathing. Sometimes when I'm alone, I still hear his voice in my head telling me what a pathetic fat loser I am." Jordan stared into the screen. "Those emotional scars don't magically go away because you're being loved by someone as fantastic as Billy."

"Billy is sort of a trigger, isn't he?" Shadow asked. Jordan nodded. "You're scared he's going to do the same thing that jerk did. You don't think you're good enough and that at any moment everything is going to come falling down."

Jordan nodded. "Exactly, and the thing is, I know he loves me, and I love him so much that I would go to the ends of the Earth for him. Hell, I disobeyed my boss and kept looking for you for Billy."

"I know that feeling," Shadow said wistfully. "I felt the same way with my husband."

Jordan laughed. "I know his name is Chris."

"How? Did he tell you?" Shadow asked, shocked.

Jordan smirked. "You did, by accident. When you were talking about Mario, you called his husband, his Chris. It wasn't hard for me to connect the dots since I knew all the players."

"Oh," Shadow sounded worried.

Jordan brushed away his tears. "Don't worry, you have to know the players in the game to figure it out. Not many people will pick up on it, and do you know how common a name Chris is?"

"True," Shadow said, relieved. "Back to what I was saying. I didn't have the emotional abuse, but all the men I loved didn't seem to love me the way I loved them. I felt I was unlovable. It made me bitter with

love. Chris disappeared on me. Brett chose porn over me. Billy didn't have the same feelings I had for him. That's why when I came back, I fought tooth and nail against falling for Chris again."

Jordan nodded. "How did you get over it? How did you open your heart?"

"I realized we were alone in the woods and I could tie his ass up if he tried to leave me," Shadow joked. Jordan's eyes went wide. "I'm kidding." Shadow then added, "Oh, yeah, I forgot what you guys have been through. Sorry."

Jordan let out a breath he didn't realize he was holding. "It's okay."

"Anyways, I realized that I needed to stop projecting my past and my fears onto Chris and deal with my feelings," Shadow answered. "I had to learn to start loving myself and letting people love me. I took it one day at a time until," Shadow let out a laugh. "Until that second kiss out in the snow."

Jordan smiled. "Chris told me to ask you about that."

"That I want on the record," Shadow responded.

Jordan nodded. "Okay, the therapy session is over."

"Oh, no," Shadow shot out. "You've got more in you that you need to get out."

Jordan sighed. "Yes. Okay, when Billy showed up at my front door, I was star-struck. He sort of just slipped into my life. We just met, and he took me to my first movie shoot. He introduced me to everyone like I was someone. Except at work, we were inseparable. He slept in my bed with me that night and didn't try anything. Then every night after that."

Jordan shook his head. "We were an old married couple before we were even boyfriends. Then that jerk Alex at that party tried to pick a fight. Then the whole first boyfriend blamed Billy for his ruined life and tried to kill him thing. I guess it was all so fast, you know?"

"I saw that video of the fight," Shadow commented. "He said some nasty things."

Jordan groaned. "Now he wants to apologize. How do I accept his apology?"

"You don't have to, but you can listen to what he has to say. It might give you some closure," Shadow answered. "As for your whirlwind romance with Billy, that means it was meant to be. Don't question it. Just go with it. The moment was right for the two of you."

Jordan thought for a moment. "Okay." He thought about what he bought Billy earlier that day. "When the moment is right."

"Are you not telling me something?" Shadow asked curiously.

Jordan smiled brightly. "No, but you did tell me what I need to do."

"Okay. Now the therapy session is over." Shadow commented. "Are you ready to hear about the second kiss out in the snow?"

Chris's voice cut in. "What are you boys talking about? Me?"

"Shadow was about to tell me about the second kiss out in the snow," Jordan answered. "Hi, Chris."

Alarmed, Chris quickly said, "I swear I didn't tell him my name."

"That's my fault, dear," Shadow responded. "Are you spreading sawdust all over my clean floors?"

Guiltily, Chis said, "Sorry."

"Go rinse off," Shadow groaned. "I'll clean up the mess after I tell Jordan about our kiss."

Chris's voice brightened. "I want to be here for that. I want to make sure you get the story right."

"You are the one that embellishes the story," Shadow chastised.

Jordan smiled to himself. They sounded like him and Billy. "Why don't we take a fifteen-minute break to let Chris get cleaned up and for me to get camera-ready?"

"That'll give me time to sweep up all the sawdust he just tracked in." Shadow sighed. "We'll talk in fifteen minutes."

20

A KISS OUT IN THE SNOW

"**H**ow do I look?" Chris's voice came over the speaker.

Jordan let out a chuckle at Shadow's groan. "We're not on camera."

"So? Can't I want to look good for my man?" Chris asked teasingly.

Shadow quipped back, "Now you want to look good for me?"

"Well, I might get a little nookie later," Chris answered.

Jordan covered his mouth to hide his laughter. He could imagine him and Billy having that same conversation.

"Your hand doesn't care what you look like," Shadow shot back playfully.

Seductively, Chris said, "So you want to watch?"

"You do know Jordan is listening to all of this, right?" Shadow asked.

Jordan uncovered his mouth. "And I'm enjoying every minute of it."

"I am here to amuse," Chris said jauntily.

Shadow playfully jabbed, "How about amusing me by picking up your dirty clothes once in a while?"

"Maybe I'm leaving you a trail to find me," Chris teased back.

Jordan cut in. "Gentlemen, while this is all very amusing, I'd like to hear about this kiss out in the snow."

"Yes, let's talk about the kiss out in the snow and how Shadow couldn't keep his hands off me," Chris said merrily.

Shadow quickly corrected him, "Excuse me? It was you that couldn't keep your hands off me."

"You used sex to get me to do what you want," Chris argued.

Shadow defended, "It was the only way to get you to do what you needed to for your recovery."

"Okay, catch me up on his recovery." Jordan leaned forward. "Are you ready for me to record?"

Chris answered, "Yes, I'll go first."

Jordan started recording. "Okay, we're recording. Go ahead, Shadow's husband. Tell us about your recovery."

"Shadow got here in September. I took my meds like I was supposed to. I went to my physical therapy. Shadow and I did my exercises together, and I bitched about the food I had to eat, but I did it all because at night I got to wrap my arms around Shadow as we slept." There was love in Chris's voice. "He even got me some simple wood carving tools for me to practice with."

Shadow added, "He'd sit on the front porch for hours trying to carve things."

"I tried carving simple things at first. They were shit," Chris continued. "I was determined, though, and I got better. It was the only thing I wanted to do. Shadow would yell at me to do my exercises or have to drag me to my appointments."

There was a slight wickedness in Shadow's voice. "I had to get creative. He needed motivation."

"He used sex," Chris said gleefully. "Eat my vegetables? I got a kiss. Do my exercises? I was supposed to get a—"

Jordan interrupted, "I get the picture."

"Oh, I don't think you do," Shadow said impishly.

Chris grumbled, "He started pushing me harder. He would tempt me with sex, but I would be too worn out to enjoy it."

"He fell for it every time," Shadow laughed. "I would touch him and he'd jerk away and yell at me not to touch him."

Chris pouted. "I hated him for it, but I loved every minute of it. I was improving. My weight got under control. Then it got cold, and we had to slow down."

"Nerve damage and cold don't go well together," Shadow explained. "His mind was willing, but his body wasn't."

Chris amended, "Well, it was willing for some things."

"We were driving each other crazy. He couldn't carve outside, so we made him a spot in the corner and laid down a tarp to catch the shavings." Shadow

sighed. "We walked around the house for an hour because we couldn't go outside and do it."

Chris huffed. "It got to the point where I was looking forward to my physical therapy appointments so I could get away from him. I would be breathing too loudly while he was watching television, or I'd get annoyed by the way he chewed."

"Before the cold hit, he could sit outside and practice his woodcarving. We could go to town and go out to eat or do something around other people. We had breaks from each other or other people," Shadow griped.

Chris added, "The real problem was that he wouldn't admit his feelings for me and I was angry at him for it. We were picking fights over the stupidest things. Then Shadow came home from getting supplies from the store. We were expecting a bad snowstorm. We weren't expecting things to explode between us."

Carrying a bag of groceries, Shadow stepped into the house to find Chris in his corner chipping away at a piece of wood. The relief at seeing Chris was okay while he was out was short-lived when he saw the state of the room. He took in a deep, calming breath.

Shadow set the groceries down on the bench they had by the door and started shedding his snow wear. He hung his coat up and tried not to let the fact the tarp they laid down for Chris's woodworking was bunched up and he was

dropping wood shavings onto the floor irritate him. He removed his snow boots and did his best not to be annoyed by Chris's dirty lunch dishes on the coffee table.

Without saying a word to Chris, he stood, picked up the groceries, and went straight to the kitchen. He saw Chris watching him, a cocky expression on his face as he purposely flicked pieces of wood onto the unprotected floor. He refused to let Chris goad him into another fight. Then he saw the state of the kitchen.

"Do you not know how to clean up after yourself?!" Shadow shouted, dropping the groceries onto the table. He put away the open loaf of bread. After pulling the knife out of the peanut butter, he cleaned it on the edge of the jar before putting it into the dishwasher. "It's not that hard!"

Shadow put away the peanut butter and chocolate syrup. He followed the drips of chocolate that started on the counter and led out into the living room. Angrily, he shouted, "Who eats peanut butter and chocolate syrup sandwiches?!"

"I do," Chris said from the doorway. "What's the big deal? I was going to put that stuff away after I finished my woodcarving."

Shadow glared at Chris. He took the dishrag from the sink and wiped the counter. "The big deal is that you dripped chocolate sauce everywhere, and you left the kitchen and living room I cleaned up before I left a mess!"

"I said I was going to clean it up after I finished my woodcarving," Chris sniped back angrily.

Shadow tossed the rag back into the sink. He focused on Chris, trying to contain his anger. "When have you ever cleaned up or picked up after yourself? You leave your clothes all over the floor in the bedroom. You couldn't put

a dish away to save your life and you get wood shavings all over the place."

"If you don't like it here, then go," Chris spat out. "You don't want to be here anyways."

Shadow grabbed one of the grocery bags and began putting things away. He snapped back, "Of course I want to be here. What I don't want is to be cleaning up after a slob all the time."

"You don't want to be here," Chris accused, leaning against the door frame. "The only reason you're here is to punish me."

Shadow glowered at Chris. "Punish you? Really?"

"Yes." Chris crossed his arms. "I get it. I hurt you when I disappeared while I was recovering. You wouldn't understand what I was going through, what I went through."

Resentment peppered Shadow's words. "You didn't give me a chance to. You made the decision for both of us. I may not have understood, but I could have been there for you."

"I only saw you when you decided to come here for your vacations." Chris pushed off the doorframe. "Do you know what it's like to get over someone and then bam they're back as if a few months prior they didn't just leave you? You broke my heart so many times, and when I got hurt, I made the decision to protect me."

Shadow crossed his arms defiantly. "Excuse me for having a life that wasn't here. I had family and school away from here."

"What was I then? Something to keep you entertained while you were here?" Chris moved in front of Shadow. "Be honest with me. Did you ever have any feelings for me? Was I just some guy to play with when you were here?"

Hurt and anger filled Shadow's voice. "How dare you?! I found every excuse to come back here to see you, and when I left, it felt like my heart was being torn out of my chest. You were the only person I could think about. Then you disappeared. Do you know what that did to me? The person I loved abandoned me."

"I abandoned you?" Chris scoffed. "I needed to heal. I'm so sorry I didn't put the person who showed up when he felt like it ahead of my own needs."

Shadow puffed up his chest defiantly. "If you would have called, I would have been here. For your injury or any other time. You know that. That's why I'm staying here with you now. To make sure you get better."

"You're here because you're too afraid to face the world. I'm just a convenient excuse for you to avoid facing everyone who would judge you for what you were doing," Chris spat out angrily.

Poking Chris in the chest, Shadow shot back. "I am not ashamed of what I did. I loved fucking on camera. I loved being an escort and being treated like a prince by my clients. I loved being Brett's boyfriend."

"Until you didn't anymore," Chris added coldly. "That's what you do. Temporarily love things. Brett. Doing porn. Being an escort. Me."

Angrily, Shadow slapped Chris across the face. "You asshole. I loved Brett, but I wasn't in love with him."

"What about me?" Chris asked bitterly. Shadow tried to move past him, but Chris wouldn't let him. "I asked, what about me?"

Shadow looked him dead in the eyes. His words were bitter. "Yes, I loved you and I still do. Happy?"

"Are you in love with me?" Chris's voice lost all its bite. Shadow tried to move past him again, but Chris blocked him. "Answer me. I know I'm in love with you. Are you in love with me?"

Angrily, Shadow answered, "I told you, I can't give you what you want."

"Can't," Chris took Shadow's hand, "or won't?"

Shadow yanked his hand back and went rigid. Sternly he said, "Can't. Stop trying to make this more than it is."

"I will when you do," Chris countered. "Don't lie to me and say you're here out of friendship. I feel how you touch me, see how you look at me, especially when we make love."

Shadow bristled. "We don't make love. We fuck."

"We make love," Chris corrected him. "Why do you keep pulling away instead of letting me in?" Chris took Shadow's hand again.

Shadow pulled his hand back again. "I'm not pulling away." He followed Chris's eyes to his hand. "I'm not doing this. All you want to do is play with your wood and have me for a little fun on the side, just like everyone else." Shadow pushed past Chris, careful not to knock him down. He shouted back, "I am tired of loving men who don't love me back!"

Shadow stormed off to their room. He was trembling with conflicting emotions. He clenched and unclenched his fists. He hated how accurate Chris was in his accusations. He let out a scream of frustration. He was angry at Chris for not understanding why he couldn't open himself up to that kind of hurt again.

"I never stopped loving you," Chris said from the doorway. He was holding something Shadow couldn't see

in his hand. Moving toward Shadow, he held it out. "It's not done, but I made this for you."

Shadow took the small wooden carving of a heart. Etched into it were his and Chris's initials, followed by 4 ever. Touched by the gift, Shadow ran a finger over the unfinished wood. "You made this for me? Why?"

"I figured if you had my heart, maybe you'd finally let me have yours," Chris answered softly.

Shadow shoved the heart back into Chris's hands. "I … I need to go."

"Where are you going?" Chris called after Shadow. "There's a snowstorm coming! It's too dangerous to go out!"

Shadow hastily put on his boots and jacket. He saw Chris coming after him. "I need to go!" he shouted at Chris before dashing out the door.

The bite of winter struck Shadow in the face. The clouds blocked the sun, casting everything in a dull gray. Falling snow was being whipped up by the wind. Shadow pulled his coat tight around him. The snow crunched under his boots when he stepped off the porch.

"Shadow!" Chris called from the front porch. "Don't go!"

Shadow turned around. Chris hadn't bothered to put on his coat or boots before coming out. He was struggling to come down the stairs, nearly falling when he reached the bottom. "What are you doing?!" Shadow shouted at him.

"I'm not letting you leave me again!" Chris wrapped his arms around himself. He stumbled forward in the snow. "What are you so afraid of?"

Shadow instinctively moved to Chris's side when he saw him stumble. "You need to go back inside."

"Not until you finally admit your feelings for me," Chris said through chattering teeth.

Shadow tried to move Chris to the door, but he refused to move. "Please, just go inside."

"Admit it," Chris demanded.

Shadow struggled with the words. Finally, he choked out, "I'm broken, Chris."

"So am I." Chris snuggled close to Shadow. "Let's be broken together."

A tear froze on Shadow's cheek as it fell. "I do love you, Chris. I do. I've been burned by love once too many times, and I … I can't handle being hurt again."

"I would never hurt you." Chris brought his lips to Shadow's. "Now kiss me so we can go back inside and warm up."

Shadow pressed his cold lips to Chris's. "Can we go inside now?"

"Gladly." Chris tugged Shadow back toward the house. "I could use a hot shower."

Shadow helped Chris up the stairs and back into the house. "You're a damn fool, you know that?" He started brushing snow off of Chris. "You know your nerves don't work well in the cold."

"I don't work well without you." Chris let Shadow sit him down on the bench. "I meant it. I'll never hurt you."

Shadow shrugged off his coat and hung it up. "I know that, but that fear is still there." He sat down and took off his boots. Chris still had his arms wrapped around himself, trying to get warm. "Chris, I'm in love with you. I have been since that first kiss. That's why this place is where my happiest memories are. They were with you."

"Then let's make some more happy memories together." Chris pulled his right arm away from himself and put it

around Shadow. "Please, stay. I'll pick up after myself, and I won't do any woodcarving until I can do it outside again."

Shadow pulled Chris up along with him. "I don't want you to stop doing your woodcarving. It's good therapy for you. As for picking up after yourself," he glanced over at the dirty dishes on the coffee table, "we both know you won't."

"I would, too," Chris protested. "For a day or two."

Shadow guided Chris to their room. "Come on, let's get into a nice hot shower and warm our bones. I can't have my boyfriend getting sick on me."

"It took me some time to let down my guard," Shadow explained. "Every time I tried to pull away, Chris pulled me right back."

Fondly, Chris said, "We got married fall of the following year. It was a simple ceremony, just family. My dad, his parents, aunt, uncle, and his little cousin."

"My parents gave us the house as a wedding present," Shadow added. "My cousin commented that we should turn this place into a bed-and-breakfast, and that's what we did."

Proudly, Chris said, "The day we got married was the happiest day of my life. I thought I was going to be the one to propose, but he surprised me."

"Shadow proposed?" Jordan asked, a little shocked. "You were the one fighting the relationship. What made you want to propose?"

The love was evident in Shadow's voice. "It wasn't one thing. I do remember looking at him one day while

he was eating one of his peanut butter and chocolate syrup sandwiches and saying to myself that this was the man I wanted to spend the rest of my life with. Then I snuck out and bought us rings."

"That was it?" Jordan asked, flabbergasted. "You weren't scared or had any doubts?"

Shadow laughed. "Of course I was scared and had my doubts. I had the rings for three weeks before I proposed. Then one day while I was watering the plants, and he was coming out of the barn covered in sawdust, it just hit me that that was the moment."

"He rushed inside and came back out right as I was coming up the stairs," Chris added fondly. "I thought he was tying his shoe when he dropped down to one knee, but then he held out a ring."

Lovingly, Shadow said, "I told him I loved him and I couldn't imagine my life without him. I told him I wanted to make our love official, so there was no doubt in either of our minds that we were going to be together forever."

"When he slipped the ring on my finger, I told him he was the love of my life and I couldn't wait to be his husband," Chris finished.

Absentmindedly, Jordan picked up his phone and looked at the wallpaper of Billy on his phone. "Marriage is such a major step."

"Having thoughts?" Shadow asked.

Jordan put his phone down. "Talking to you two really has made me think about my relationship with Billy."

"Good or bad?" Chris asked.

Jordan smiled. "Good."

EXIT INTERVIEW

"**T**HANK YOU SO much for talking to Alex." Cameron beamed on Jordan's screen. "I hope everyone else can be as forgiving."

Jordan thought about that word, forgiving. He hoped Billy would forgive him for the hurt he was about to cause him and smiled warmly back at Cameron. "He was genuinely sorry and there's no point in holding onto that anger."

"You're different," Cameron commented. "You look relaxed and you have this glow."

Jordan laughed. "Are you saying I was stressed out before?"

"Honestly? Yes," Cameron said bluntly. "You almost never take time off, and when you do, you're working on something."

A warm smile brightened Jordan's face. "I'm looking forward to seeing Billy and spending some alone time with him."

"That's so sweet and a huge ass lie." Cameron studied Jordan through the screen. "Dish, bitch."

Unphased by the callout, Jordan said, "Have you ever thought how lucky we are to have met Billy and Carlos?"

"You might be lucky. I'm cursed," Cameron huffed.

Jordan shook his head. "Cameron, put yourself in Carlos's shoes. How would you feel if he was calling and texting his ex and wouldn't tell you what it's about? Then you fly out to see him without an explanation?"

"Okay," Cameron grumbled. "But—"

Jordan cut him off. "No buts. Carlos's feelings are his, and they're valid. You need to talk to him. Don't ruin what you have because you won't admit how you feel about him."

"Alex and Owen said the same thing," Cameron said, rolling his eyes. "That doesn't explain this change in you," Cameron smirked. "I think it's your exit interview time."

Jordan let out a groan. "Do we have to?"

"They aren't my rules. They're the rules of the great and almighty Jordan Hudson," Cameron teased. "Ready?"

Jordan clicked record. "We're recording."

"Jordan, you've finished your interview with Shadow, correct?" Cameron asked in his reporter's voice.

Jordan smirked, knowing his answer was going to throw Cameron off. "No. I've finished my interview with Shadow and his husband."

"Hold on, you interviewed them both?" Cameron asked, trying to keep his composure.

Jordan mentally cheered Cameron for not faltering too badly. "Yeah, at first I thought it was Shadow's story I was needing, and it turned out it was both of theirs."

"You said that *you* needed, not what Billy needed. Why?" Cameron stared intently through the screen, waiting for the answer.

Jordan mentally cheered and jeered Cameron for catching that. "Are you sure you're ready for the answer?"

"You're stalling," Cameron responded tersely.

Jordan's face went serious. "I'm finally being honest with myself. Why not be honest with the world, right?"

"Did I cross a line?" Cameron asked, concerned.

Jordan shook his head. "No, I led you there. You just followed the trail."

"Alright. You brought us here. Tell us what you have to say," Cameron said, focusing on Jordan.

Jordan looked into the camera and not at Cameron. "Billy knows this. The rest of you may have guessed it. I have body image issues. I've always been a bigger guy, wanting to be a smaller guy. Being a gay man, I'm part of one tribe while wanting to be part of another."

"I've had my suspicions," Cameron admitted.

Jordan nodded. "What only Billy knew was that before him, I had a boyfriend who preyed on those insecurities. He nearly broke me. I had even stopped writing."

"Oh, Jordan," Cameron commented.

Jordan held up a hand to stop him from continuing. "Billy came into my life, and he loved me for who I was. He inspired me to write again. I couldn't believe someone like Billy wanted to be with me. Then we were together, and it was amazing. For a while."

"What happened?" Cameron asked.

Jordan wiped a tear from his cheek. "The reality of it. I look like me, and Billy looks like Billy. Even with Billy reassuring me, those doubts and voices crept back into my head. I kept waiting for Billy to leave me."

"Billy would never leave you," Cameron commented.

Jordan wiped away his tears. "I know that, but, subconsciously, the fear is still there. I also was quietly hurting Billy because I was holding back my affection for him."

"What changed or did it?" Cameron asked.

Jordan looked into Cameron's eyes on the screen. "I talked to Shadow, then his husband, and then they told me their story."

"Talking to them changed you?" Cameron asked in disbelief.

Jordan nodded. "It helped me see that I need to work on me and my issues like they did with theirs."

"How are you going to do that?" Cameron asked, concern slipping into his voice.

Jordan sighed. "Therapy. I'm also going to make a conscious effort to accept Billy's public displays of affection. I'm also going to get healthy physically."

"You said get healthy not skinny. Is there a difference?" Cameron pointed out.

Jordan smiled, happy that Cameron picked up on his lead. "There is. You can be skinny and unhealthy. Being healthy is about eating right, making sure my body has proper nutrition, and strengthening my body properly. I'll never have a body like yours or like Billy's, but I can have a healthy body I'm happy with for me."

"You got all that from your interview with Shadow and his husband?" Cameron asked curiously.

Jordan fidgeted a moment before answering. "I did. Shadow called me out about my lack of showing affection for Billy in public. Then, as I heard their story, it hit me that, like Shadow, I kept a part of myself locked away. He had to work on himself to be able to open up to his husband, who never gave up on loving him, just like Billy does with me."

"Speaking of Billy, how do you think he's going to react to the news about you finding Shadow?" Cameron asked. Jordan saw the regret in his eyes for asking.

Jordan hugged himself. "He's going to be over-joyed that I found him. Then he's going to break down when I tell him that Shadow doesn't want to be found by him, and I can't tell him how to contact Shadow."

"Can't or won't?" Cameron quickly asked.

Jordan looked away for a moment, then back at Cameron on the screen before he lied. "Can't. The only way I have to contact Shadow is via an email address he's already closed. Even if I wanted to, I couldn't help Billy contact Shadow."

"Even if you wanted to," Cameron repeated. "What does that mean?"

Jordan shrugged. "Exactly what that means. I have to respect Shadow's wishes. He doesn't want Billy to contact him and he doesn't want to be thrust out into the spotlight again. If I betray the trust he has in me to protect his privacy, then how will anyone ever be able to trust me again? If Billy connects with Shadow again, it'll be because of someone else, not me."

"Then the only way Billy is going to get to hear from Shadow is through your interview?" Cameron asked.

Jordan's face brightened. "No. Shadow filmed a personal video for Billy. With his husband. I'm hoping it will give Billy what he needs."

"Have you seen that video?" Cameron asked curiously.

Jordan shook his head. "No. That video is for Billy, and if Billy chooses to share it with me, that will be up to him."

"What's next for Jordan Hudson?" Cameron asked with a devious smile.

Jordan chose his words carefully. "If everything goes well with Billy finding out about Shadow, I have a joint project I'm going to propose to him. I also plan on taking some time off to work on me, and get back to my writing roots."

"For the record, I'm here for you if you need me," Cameron said wholeheartedly. "You're more than my best friend. You're family. Whatever you need, I'm here for you. I mean it. So is the rest of your second family."

Jordan felt the love in his words. "I know, and I love you all for it." Jordan ended the recording. "I am so scared that Billy is going to leave me over this."

"Billy will never leave you," Cameron responded, his voice full of compassion. "He loves you."

Jordan laughed. "And everyone loves Billy. Did I ever tell you about Billy meeting my parents? It was amazing. We were dating for a month, and everything was blowing up about the Country Boyz. I didn't even get a chance to tell them I was dating Billy before they heard it on the news."

"That sucks," Cameron commented. "How did they feel about it?"

Jordan smiled. "They were more than a little bothered about Billy's line of work and my new career path. They wanted to meet him, though. I booked us a flight. We stayed with my parents, in my old bedroom, in fact." Jordan shook his head in disbelief. "Billy met them for five minutes and had them won over. They had him calling them mom and dad before we left."

"That's amazing." Cameron smiled.

Jordan's eyes began to water. "That's why if Billy leaves me, it will hurt so much. He won't just be breaking up with me but with my family as well. Do you know how excited he was when we went to see them for the holidays? How excited they were to see him? I can't lose him, Cameron. I can't."

"He's not going to leave you," Cameron reassured him.

Jordan wiped away at his eyes. "Can you promise me that?"

"I can absolutely promise you that." Cameron winked at him. "Just like I can guarantee Billy will say yes to that joint project you plan on proposing to him."

IF THE PORCH IS A ROCKIN

S HADOW PICKED AT the dead leaves on his hanging plants. Inspiration hit Chris, and he was busy in the barn working on a project. He was only coming out covered in a layer of sweat and sawdust when he needed to for his food, medicine, or sleep. Shadow knew from experience there was no dissuading him once the muses took hold of him.

It had been one day since their last video interview with Jordan. He missed his conversations with Jordan, rehashing the past and getting to know the man who held Billy's delicate heart. He had expected the interviews to be rough. He hadn't expected the unspoken friendship they developed.

"You okay?" Chris startled Shadow by placing a hand on his shoulder.

Shadow turned around to see his lover and burst out into laughter upon seeing his lover covered in sawdust. "Did you bathe in sawdust?"

"I may have gotten a bit dusty." Chris combed his hand through his hair with his hand, showering the ground with sawdust.

Shadow brushed at Chris's clothes. "You are not going into the house like that. You're stripping outside and rinsing off with the water hose."

"What about the squirrels?" Chris asked seriously.

Puzzled, Shadow asked, "The squirrels? What about them?"

Chris grinned cheekily. "They might try to go after my nuts."

"They'll have to fight me for them." Shadow playfully punched him. "What are you working on in there?"

Vaguely, Chris answered, "It's a special collection." He took Shadow's hand. "What about you? Trying to keep busy so you don't miss talking to Jordan?"

"I wanted to hate him because he was with Billy, but I ended up liking him. I'm grateful Billy found such a great guy." Shadow started unzipping Chris's coveralls.

Chris let Shadow pull off his overalls. "You know you can still reach out to him. You did tell him you'd leave the email account active until after he told Billy."

"I know, but I don't want to get used to just calling him." Shadow tugged down the overalls to Chris's waist. "I do want him to be able to reach out to me if, for some reason, things with him and Billy don't go well."

Chris kicked off his shoes. "You want to be there for him. I get it."

"I don't want to be the instrument of their breakup." Shadow bent over and pulled the overalls down.

With a hand on Shadow's shoulder, Chris pulled one leg out. "Do you want to see Billy?"

"I do." Shadow pulled the overalls off the other leg. "I don't want the drama that it could bring, though."

Chris pulled off his undershirt. "What if it didn't bring all the drama?"

"I know you want to meet Billy and Jordan." Shadow draped the overalls over the porch rail. "Maybe one day they'll show up at our front door. Maybe one day I'll be ready to call Jordan and arrange a meeting."

Chris dropped his shorts and kicked them aside. "Don't wait too long. Talking to Jordan helped you work through a lot of your personal demons. I know it was hard, but you look happier."

"Yeah." Shadow admired his husband standing on the front porch in just a pair of socks. "You know what would make me really happy?"

Chris winked at him. "A little porch sex?"

"If you would take your socks off so I can rinse you off. That way, you can go inside and take a real shower before we have dinner," Shadow teased.

Chris took hold of the rail and lifted one foot at a time to pull off his socks. He tossed them at Shadow. "You're no fun anymore."

"I'm plenty of fun." Shadow smacked Chris's ass as he headed to the stairs. "Now hurry up. I'm hungry."

Stepping carefully down the stairs, Chris said, "You can always eat my ass if you're hungry."

"Maybe after your shower, I'm not going to get a splinter in my tongue," Shadow joked back.

Chris turned around and raised his arms to his side. "I'm ready for you to squirt me with your hose."

"Smart ass." Shadow picked up the hose and turned on the water. He started spraying water on Chris. "Don't think you're going to drip water all over the floors. You're going to wait out here until I bring you a towel."

Chris spun around so Shadow could rinse his back. "I'll be out here waiting, letting all my bits and pieces dangle about."

"Don't scare the birds or you won't get any of the brownies I got from the store." Shadow lowered the hose. Happy with his work, he turned the water off and coiled the hose back up. "I'll be right back with a towel."

Chris shook the water from his hair. "I'll be waiting."

Shadow headed inside. He went into the bedroom, and he paused a moment at his computer. He fought the urge to turn it on and video call Jordan. It wasn't only to regain his connection to Billy. He truly liked Jordan. Their conversations were cathartic and knowing Billy had Jordan was reassuring.

Pushing those desires aside, Shadow grabbed a towel from their bathroom, then returned to the porch. He found Chris leaning over the rail, arching his back so his plump ass jutted out. The water on his skin sparkled in the sunlight. It was an alluring and enticing sight.

Lost in thought, Chris didn't hear Shadow move up behind him. Dropping the towel, Shadow fell to his knees behind his husband. Burying his face between Chris's plump cheeks, Shadow rapidly whipped his

tongue about. Chris jumped with surprise, then pushed his butt back with a groan.

"I thought you said you were hungry," Chris teased, looking back at his lover.

Pulling back for a moment, Shadow playfully slapped one of Chris's cheeks. "I thought you said I could eat your ass."

"By all means, be my guest." Chris leaned farther over the rail, thrusting his ass back.

Shadow returned to devouring Chris's ass, swirling his tongue along the sensitive skin. He massaged Chris's furry cheeks as he pulled them farther apart to dive deeper, to let his tongue rapidly swipe across the perfect pucker. He felt Chris's body tremble with pleasure.

Shadow squeezed Chris's cheeks before pulling away to pull off his shirt. Christ turned around and leaned back against the railing. Shadow pounced on his jutting cock, swallowing it down to the base with ease. Chris tossed his head back and let out a groan.

"You really do know how to make a man feel special," Chris moaned in delight.

Shadow worked Chris's cock eagerly, sliding his tongue along the underside of the shaft. His left hand went to play with Chris's balls, the other he slipped behind Chris to stroke his hole. Chris ran his hand through Shadow's hair, then started thrusting his hips forward to fuck Shadow's mouth.

"Baby, oh, baby," Chris moaned, pumping his cock into Shadow's mouth.

Shadow pulled off his cock. Looking up at his husband, Shadow licked his lips. "Still think I'm no fun?"

"What I think is you have too many clothes on." Chris reached down and pulled Shadow to his feet. Shadow kicked off his shoes while Chris fumbled with his pants. Kissing Shadow, he shoved the pants down Shadow's thighs. "Remind me to never complain about you being frisky ever again."

With Shadow's help, Chris went to his knees. He tugged Shadow's pants off his legs, then tossed them aside. He grinned up at Shadow, then swallowed him down. Shadow ran his hand through Chris's drying hair. He let out a grumbly growl at the feel of Chris's warm, welcoming mouth.

He looked down at his husband, who was enjoying his cock with lustful, loving eyes. He watched his cock slide in and out of Chris's hungry mouth. His body tingled from Chris's fingertips dancing up and down the back of his thighs. Shadow felt the sexual urges exploding in him.

"Over the railing," Shadow growled, lifting Chris to his feet. "I want that ass."

"Yeah, baby. Fuck me good." With his legs spread and ass sticking out, Chris leaned over the railing.

Shadow spit on his cock, then on Chris's hole. He rubbed his cock head over Chris's hole. "You want this dick, baby?" Shadow teased.

"Yes." Chris pushed back, trying to impale himself on Shadow's cock.

Shadow tapped his dick on Chris's ass. "You're an eager bottom today."

"Quit teasing me or get me a toy," Chris snarled back at Shadow.

Shadow pushed the head of his cock into Chris, causing the man to groan with satisfaction. "Your wish is my command." Shadow held onto Chris's hip as he inched his way into him. "I love the way my cock feels with you wrapped around it."

"Save the sweet talk for the bedroom," Chris growled. "Fuck me, already."

Shadow started pumping his cock into his lover. Slowly at first but he quickly picked up speed. Shadow pulled Chris back by the shoulders so they were chest to back. Shadow sucked on the back of Chris's neck, causing him to moan with delight. Shadow put one arm around Chris's waist. With his free hand, he started stroking Chris's cock.

"Do it, baby! Fuck me!" Chris cried out.

Shadow grunted. He grazed his teeth over the skin on Chris's neck. He thrust harder into his lover while holding Chris tighter against him. Both of their bodies began to shake with their impending climaxes. Shadow sank his teeth into Chris's neck, careful not to break the skin.

"I'm cumming!" Chris cried out as his cock blew his seed all over the railing and into the yard.

Shadow's dick exploded in Chris. He squeezed Chris tighter, nearly crushing the air out of him. He punched his cock up into Chris, milking the last few drops out of his balls, and kissed the bite mark on Chris's skin as he pumped the last few drops from Chris's cock. Then he nuzzled the back of Chris's neck.

"Sorry. I couldn't resist when I saw you standing out here naked," Shadow sighed.

Chris leaned back into him. "Wasn't it my turn to fuck you?"

"You can fuck me twice tonight," Shadow laughed, kissing the back of Chris's neck. "I left a mark on your neck."

Chris groaned. "You know it's too hot for turtlenecks."

"It's below the collar." Shadow squeezed him tighter.

Chris rocked them back and forth. "Normally I love our after-sex cuddles, but I am getting hungry."

"Just a minute longer," Shadow sighed. "I really need to hold you right now."

Chris patted Shadow's hand. "Take as long as you need."

"I hope Billy doesn't get too upset with Jordan," Shadow commented.

Chris turned around in Shadow's arms. "I have a feeling they are going to be okay."

"I hope so." Shadow rubbed his nose against Chris's. "I hope so."

Chris started laughing. "I finally painted the railing."

23

WHOOPS!

"WHAT DID YOU think of that video of Paris with the sexy twunk?" Cameron asked over the speakerphone.

Jordan held up a shirt, then tossed it on the bed. "I thought it was great. Paris and that guy—what's his name? Danny? Have great chemistry together."

"They do. I hope they still do the show after what happened with Mark," Cameron commented.

Jordan paused and looked at his phone. "What happened to Mark?"

"Billy hasn't told you?" Cameron asked, surprised.

Jordan shook his head, then realized Cameron couldn't see him. "No, every time I call Billy, he sends me to voicemail, then sends me a text saying he misses me and he'll call me when he gets a chance."

"Then you don't know what all has happened," Cameron sounded regretful. "The wedding has been called off."

Jordan stared at the phone. "What?! What happened?!"

"The gist of it is, there were a series of events that were threatening the wedding. Paris put out all the fires, but they were getting to Mark and then he fired Paris over that cooking twunk," Cameron explained. "Aunt Lexi called me a little while ago and told me everything."

Picking up the phone, Jordan sat down on the bed. "Should I stop packing?"

"Keep packing. No way Paris is going to let this wedding not happen. Besides, we have to make our announcements to everyone." Cameron groaned. "We also need to collect our boyfriends. Apparently, they have been getting into mischief."

Jordan smiled. "That's my Billy."

"Your Billy is encouraging my Carlos to be naughty," Cameron chided him.

Jordan beamed. "You called him your Carlos. Does that mean you two have made up?"

"Not yet," Cameron grumbled. "He and Billy are either trying to get Hunter out of his room or console Mark. I'm not sure. Aunt Lexi said it's a madhouse there."

Jordan set the phone back on the nightstand and got off the bed. "Do you think everything is going to work out with Mark and Hunter?"

"Yeah, those two were made for each other." Amused, Cameron said, "They are the only two I know that fornicate more than you and Billy."

Jordan pulled out a pair of jeans. "Look at you, using big words." Jordan put the jeans back in the

closet. "Billy and I don't, as you put it, fornicate more than anyone else."

"All I know is your bedroom is going to be right next to my bedroom. I don't want you keeping me up or waking me with your moans and groans," Cameron ordered. He then added, "And I don't want Billy and Carlos to have 'who can be louder during sex' contests."

Jordan pulled a pair of slacks from the closet. "We won't keep you up or wake you up when we get amorous." Jordan hung the slacks back up. "Wait, what are you talking about? We don't live next to each other."

"Um, whoops," Cameron responded, sounding regretful. "Forget I said anything."

Jordan's tone grew serious. "Cameron, spill it."

"Fine, but you didn't hear it from me," Cameron relented. "It's supposed to be a surprise. The condo next to mine is going on the market, and Billy wants to buy it. For the two of you."

Dumbfounded, Jordan blurted out, "What? We have a place. Two places, in fact. Why does he want to get us a third place?" Jordan paused. Fear gripped him. "Are you sure it's for us or just him?"

"Jordan, stop it. It's for the both of you," Cameron admonished. "You should have heard him talking about it. It's a three-bedroom like mine. He was planning on turning one into a shared office for you two, one for his fan content, and creating you a writing nook so he can quietly watch you while you create."

Jordan smiled warmly. "You know, the only time he's quiet and calm is when he watches me write? Snacks and drinks magically appear beside me. He does so much for me, and I do nothing for him."

"Are you kidding? You do everything for him that he needs," Cameron scolded. "With you he's Billy. Not Billy, the porn star. Not Billy, the guy who survived the Country Boyz murders. He's Billy. You give him that sense of normalcy he needs, and you put up with his craziness."

Jordan laughed. "I love his craziness. He takes me out of my comfort zone, and I keep him reined in."

"Then why did you go to Billy was getting the condo for himself?" Cameron asked pointedly.

Jordan fell back on the bed. "I'm worried about what will happen after I tell Billy about Shadow. It could break us."

"Or make you stronger," Cameron commented. "He's going to hurt, but you're going to show him all that footage, right? And didn't Shadow make him a personal video? He's going to see all that and understand. I promise you."

Jordan sat back up. "How did the guy not talking to his boyfriend get so wise?"

"You do realize I'm dating Carlos, right?" Cameron mocked.

Jordan chuckled. "Yes, so the real question is, do you like him or hate him this week?"

"I love to hate him," Cameron laughed.

Jordan thought for a moment. "You know, I get that. I know he drives you crazy and you hate how he gets jealous. You also love it, though. He keeps your life interesting, and that jealousy reassures you that he loves you."

"He calls me chipmunk. Chipmunk. Do you know why he calls me chipmunk?" Cameron groaned.

Jordan grinned wickedly. "Because you want his nut between your cheeks." Jordan paused, then added, "Both sets."

"Oh, my God. How many people has he told that to?" Cameron asked exasperated.

Jordan did his best to contain his laughter. "That I know of, just Billy, who told me."

"At least you got a normal pet name. Teddy Bear," Cameron sighed.

Jordan smiled, remembering the significance of the pet name. "When we go to sleep, he snuggles against me and calls me his Teddy Bear. I love it when we snuggle." Jordan's eyes went wide. Inspiration hit him. "I finally found the perfect pet name for Billy."

"Are you going to share?" Cameron asked curiously.

Jordan got up off the bed. "Naw, I want him to hear it first." Jordan went back to his closet. "Okay, so we're still going to a wedding that may or may not happen. We're going to announce our projects that are going to upset everyone, and the stars of the cooking show pilot we loved, may or may not do it now? Does that sum it all up?"

"Pretty much." Cameron laughed. "You know it's going to all end happily ever after. It always does, doesn't it?"

Jordan pulled out a yellow shirt with a black zigzag across the waist area. "Normally." Jordan threw the shirt into a growing pile on the floor. "When we get back, you're taking me shopping."

"You really are making changes. I've been trying to get you to go shopping with me for ages." Cameron

mischievously asked, "Is it just clothes or are we doing skincare and makeup, too?"

"The works." Jordan pulled out an oversized graphic tee that was too big for him. He was about to toss it onto the pile, then put it back. He thought to himself, *Maybe Billy can sleep in this when he's out of town. It might help him sleep.*

Cameron's voice broke his thoughts of Billy just wearing the oversized shirt. "Okay, I need to go. I'll see you tomorrow. Remember, we're going to the hotel, not the house. Our tuxes are there. I'll text you any updates on the wedding."

"I remember." Jordan pulled out a pair of jeans, debated, then put them back. "Thank you for everything, Cameron. I couldn't make it through this without you."

Cameron's voice was full of sincerity. "Hey, you're more than a friend. Your family. No matter what, you'll always be family to me. I'll see you tomorrow."

"Tomorrow," Jordan said softly to himself, "you're only a day away."

THE WEDDING ANNOUNCEMENT

"**C**AMERON, I WANT you beside Jordan all night," Lexi ordered. She was looking in the mirror, putting the finishing touches on her makeup. "Jordan, keep a lid on everything until after the wedding. I'll gather the family for a private toast."

Jordan tugged at his collar. "I promise I won't do anything that will ruin the wedding."

"Are you guys sure me and Owen should be going?" Alex asked nervously. "I'm not exactly on good terms with everyone else."

Lexi put on her earrings. "Hunter wants you there. I double-checked with him and Mark today."

"It'll be okay. If Carlos gives you any problems, I'll handle him," Cameron reassured him.

Jordan made a face in thought. "You know, if you think about it. They should all be thanking you."

"What?" Alex asked in disbelief. "Why?"

Jordan shrugged. "If you hadn't taken Dennis out that night, he wouldn't have heard that noise, and they wouldn't have gotten the cameras, and he wouldn't have met Benjamin."

"That's a stretch," Alex commented.

Jordan then added, "Well, if you hadn't confronted Billy at the party, Billy probably wouldn't have admitted his feelings for me. Cameron wouldn't have broken up with you and then wouldn't have gone to Walden Woods and met Carlos."

"I hate how your mind works," Cameron laughed. "I never thought about that. Alex is the reason we are all dating who we are."

Alex fidgeted. "It doesn't excuse me for being such an asshole."

"You are what you eat," Owen teased. "That's why I'm such a dick."

Jordan laughed. "I like you, Owen. You're really going to fit into this goofball family."

"Okay, boys." Lexi stood up and faced them. "We've got a wedding to attend."

Jordan hated not being with Billy at the reception. He could tell Cameron was feeling the same way about Carlos. When they had gotten to the house, Lexi had kept them separated until it was time to walk down the aisle as a groomsman. Billy had kissed him on the lips softly before taking his arm and walking down the aisle with him. After the ceremony, Cameron had whisked him away.

"I don't know if I can do it," Jordan said nervously. "I know I can't keep it from him, but I don't know if I can tell him either."

Cameron put an arm around him. "You can do this. We're all here for you and Billy."

"I sure hope so." Jordan took in a deep breath and let it out.

Lexi strolled up. "Boys, it's time. Go get your men."

"Why are we boys, and they are men?" Cameron asked cheekily, crossing his arms.

Lexi tweaked his nose. "Because you two belong to me, they belong to Hunter and Mark." She looked at Jordan. "Are you ready?"

"As ready as I'll ever be." Jordan felt his stomach twist with anxiety.

Lexi took Jordan's hand and gave it a squeeze. "It'll be okay. I promise. Now, go get your men. I'll meet you inside."

"Shall we?" Cameron asked after Lexi left.

Jordan nodded. "Let's do this."

Paris casually strolled up to them as they crossed the backyard. "I'm glad you two are finally here. Your boyfriends are terrors."

"Tell me about it. My Latin Lover does make me laugh, though." Cameron chuckled.

Jordan grinned. "I heard your attack twunk put them in their place. Did he really chase them out of the kitchen with a butcher's knife?"

"Spatula." Paris laughed.

"Teddy Bear!" Billy wrapped his arms around Jordan. Billy lifted him up and spun him around in the air. He set Jordan down and started babbling excitedly.

"Did Paris tell you about topping his big dick twunk boyfriend? You got to see his dick! It's massive! It's bigger than Carlos's."

Jordan was overtaken with desire upon seeing Billy's exuberant face and he took Billy by the face and kissed him, silencing his rambling. Billy put his arms around him and kissed him back. Jordan couldn't believe he was actually kissing Billy in public and that he initiated it.

"I love you, Billy," Jordan whispered to him.

Laughing, Paris asked, "Is that how you get him to shut up?"

"Hey, Chipmunk," Carlos said, taking Cameron's hand. His voice was soft and apologetic. "I missed you."

Cameron's words came out angrier than he expected. "You could have come over and talked to me." Gentling his voice, he added, "Look, I know you think something's going on with me and Alex, but that's been long over between us. He was going through some stuff and needed my help. I'm with you, Latin Lover."

"I know. I was just being jealous." Carlos kissed Cameron gently.

Jordan reluctantly let go of Billy. "Anyways, boys, we're all needed in the living room for a special toast. Then Lexi wants us to tell you what Cameron and I were up to."

"Wait! You can tell us what you two were doing now?! Tell me! Tell me! Tell me!" Billy exclaimed, jumping up and down excitedly.

Jordan kissed Billy again. It felt good to show his affection toward Billy in public. "Calm down or I'll get Daniel's spatula."

Billy pouted. "It was a butcher's knife."

"Sure it was, Pookie." Jordan patted Billy's cheek. "Now go get Ryan and Caleb, then meet us in the living room."

Cameron turned to Paris. "Paris, will you grab Daniel? Lexi said she wants the whole family there."

After Cameron's shocking announcement, Jordan took Billy's hand. He gave it a squeeze, then pulled Billy to the center with him. He looked deep into Billy's loving eyes. He had to do this. He knew it was going to hurt Billy, but not knowing or finding out from someone else would hurt far worse.

Jordan saw that everyone still had their attention focused on Cameron, Alex, and Owen. He straightened his back. "Guys! Focus! Or I'll have Daniel take a spatula to you all!"

Jordan waited until the laughter died down. He took Billy's hand in his. He took a deep breath. "Billy, after I wrote that article about you and the Country Boyz killings, there's been a lot of speculation about what happened to Shadow."

Confused, Billy said, "Yeah, you said you couldn't find him. He simply vanished. No one can find him. We gave up months ago."

"That's because he didn't want to be found." Jordan felt his heart racing. He saw Lexi behind Billy, motioning him on. "He still doesn't."

Billy shook his head. "I don't understand."

Jordan looked at Lexi for strength. He turned his attention back to Billy. A chill ran down his body when he spoke. "I know what happened to Shadow." He watched Billy's eyes grow wide. "He contacted me, and while you were here, I was video-interviewing him. He wanted to share his story in hopes people will finally stop looking for him."

Billy became frantic. "Where is he? Where is he?"

"He's living a quiet life now. With his husband." It was breaking Jordan's heart to see how upset he was making Billy. "He told me to tell you that he loves you and when he's ready, he'll contact you."

Tears trickled down his cheeks. "You got to tell me."

"I wish I could." Jordan squeezed his hands. He pulled Billy into a hug, remembering his promise to Shadow. "I wish I could."

Jordan held Billy tightly. They sank to the floor. Billy pleaded, "Please, tell me."

"Guys, let's give these two a moment alone," Lexi said to everyone.

Billy wept into Jordan's chest. "Why won't you tell me?"

"I would if I could." Jordan stroked Billy's back. "Hurting you is the last thing I want to do." Tears began running down his face. "I brought all the footage and organized it for you to watch." Billy shook in his arms. "He made a personal video for you."

Billy squeezed Jordan tight. "I want to see it all." He pulled away to look Jordan in the face. "Right now."

TUESDAY, 3 AM

FALLING IN AND out of sleep, Jordan lay in the bed restlessly. Carlos went with Cameron to the hotel so Jordan would have a bed to sleep in when Billy finally came out of his bedroom. He understood why Billy was upset, but that didn't ease the fear that he may have lost Billy by giving him what he needed: closure.

Jordan stared at the time on the clock. It was three in the morning on a Tuesday. The bedroom door opened. Billy's silhouette stood in the doorway. Jordan held his breath, waiting to see what he would do. It seemed like an eternity before Billy stepped in, closing the door behind him.

Jordan rolled onto his side, his back to Billy. He listened to Billy undress. He felt the bed dip when Billy climbed into the bed. Jordan waited, doing his best not to say anything. For the first time in a long while, Jordan was at a loss for words. What Billy would do in the next moments would tell him everything.

Jordan felt Billy moving in the bed. Billy curled his body around him. Jordan finally let out his breath when he felt Billy's arm wrap around him. Billy snuggled up against Jordan. His breath tickled the back of Jordan's neck. Jordan cautiously moved his hand to take Billy's. Their fingers intertwined.

"I love you, Teddy Bear," Billy whispered in his ear. "After watching what you filmed, I get it. I'll respect Shadow's wishes."

Jordan's eyes began to water. "I love you, too, Snuggles."

"Snuggles?" Billy squeezed him close. "I like that."

Jordan squeezed Billy's hand. "Did you watch the video Shadow made for you?"

"No, I want to watch it with you in the morning." Billy kissed him on the cheek. "Right now, I just want to fall asleep holding you."

Jordan smiled. "I can be the big spoon if you want."

"Not tonight." Billy settled into the bed. "I don't want to let you go."

Billy sat down on the bed in his bedroom at Mark's and Hunter's house. "Will you do something for me?" Billy asked, watching Jordan pull Shadow's video up on his laptop.

"If it's that thing you wanted to do that I said no to before, the answer is still no." Jordan smiled back. "What is it?"

Billy grinned. "Not that. The parts of the interview where you and Shadow talk about us, leave that in."

"Are you sure?" Jordan sat beside him.

Billy put his arm around Jordan. "Yes. I know the interview is long and you have to take some stuff out, but keep that in. Please?"

"I will." Jordan leaned into Billy. "Will you do something for me, Snuggles?"

"I like that name." Billy beamed. "What is it, Teddy Bear?"

Jordan sighed. "Let's go away, just the two of us to someplace quiet, someplace where we can be us."

"I'd like that." Billy pulled Jordan close. "I'm ready."

Jordan reached over and started the video. His eyes grew wide when he saw that the camera was on. Shadow sat there with his husband, Chris. He hadn't expected Shadow to show his face. Billy reached out and touched the screen. Jordan looked at Billy. He saw the smile and tears in his eyes. Billy pulled his hand back.

"Hey, Billy," Shadow said into the camera. "Hey, Jordan. I assume he's there with you, Billy, or you'll let him watch this video." Shadow smiled. "You've got yourself a good man. You're a lucky man." Shadow put his arm around Chris. "This is my husband, Chris. I'm a lucky man, too."

Chris waved at the screen. "Hey, Billy. Hey, Jordan. I can't wait to meet you in person."

"One day," Shadow cut in. "I do miss you, Billy. I do want to see you again. When I'm ready." Shadow side-bumped Chris. "We have Jordan's contact information. Thank you again, Jordan, for doing this, for

Billy and me. I hope my story helps you, Billy. I hope it helped you understand why I had to disappear and never look back."

Shadow bit his lower lip. "I hope you don't hold it against me for tricking you into that last scene that never was a scene. I hope you're not angry that I jump-started your career the way I did. I knew you were destined to be a star, but not if you stayed there.

"I'm happy, Billy." Shadow looked at his husband, then back to the camera. "I'm living a good, quiet life that makes me happy. I know you want to see me and pick me up in some great big hug and spin me around. I promise one day you will, but know that I am happy. Just like I know you're happy with Jordan."

Chris looked at Shadow and then at the camera. "He is happy, Billy. I assure you. He makes me happy, too. Thank you for being his friend." Chris smiled brightly. "I'll take care of him, like he takes care of me." He winked at the camera. "I'll work on him about meeting you because I want to meet you."

"You see what I have to live with?" Shadow laughed. "I love you, Billy. This is goodbye for now."

Billy wiped his eyes when the video ended. "Thank you for having him do that for me."

"I would do anything for you, Billy." Jordan put his arms around Billy.

Mischievously, Billy asked, "Anything?"

"I'll do anything for love, but I won't do that," Jordan laughed. "We better go get some breakfast. I think I heard Cameron and Carlos come in."

Billy stood up, pulling Jordan to his feet. "If he eats all the bacon, I swear."

"Go, I'll be there in a minute." Jordan pecked Billy on the cheek. Billy winked at him, then rushed out of the room.

Jordan waited a moment before sneaking out of the room and heading to the room they slept in the night before. He went to his carry-on bag and found what he was looking for. Closing his eyes, he clutched it to his chest. He smiled. He knew this was the right time.

In the kitchen, he found Billy sitting with Cameron, Carlos, and Alex. Paris was chatting with Lexi and Owen. Mark and Hunter were laughing with Benjamin and Dennis. Daniel was cooking. Brad and Cody were whispering to each other, probably trying to sneak away.

"How's it going, kiddo?" Caleb asked, putting a hand on Jordan's shoulder. "Everything good?"

Jordan smiled at seeing Caleb with his arm around Ryan. "Yeah, great."

"I'm famished. I worked up a real hunger last night." Ryan winked at Jordan before pulling Caleb to the crowded table.

Jordan took a moment to take in everyone all together. *This is my family*, he thought.

"Teddy Bear, I saved you a seat." Billy patted his leg.

Jordan laughed. He walked over to Billy. He took Billy's hand and pulled him to his feet. "I love you, Billy."

"I love you, too, Jordan," Billy responded, a little confused.

Jordan shook his head, the happiness in him ready to explode. He noticed the table grew silent. He felt

everyone's eyes on them. "Billy, since the first day I met you, you have turned my life upside down and I've loved every minute of it. You believed in me when I didn't. You make me smile and laugh. You've made me a better person."

Letting go of Billy's hand, Jordan dropped to one knee. He pulled out the tiny box and opened it, revealing a gold band with a single diamond in it. "I want to spend the rest of my life with you. Will you marry me?"

"Yes!" Billy cried out, tears of joy pouring down his face. He dropped to his knees and hugged Jordan. "Yes! Yes! Yes! A million times, yes!"

The table erupted in cheers. Jordan squeezed Billy tight, then pulled back to pluck the ring from the box. With trembling hands, he slipped the ring onto Billy's finger. Billy held his hand up to look at it, then hugged Jordan again, nearly causing the two to fall to the ground.

"I'm not planning their wedding!" Jordan heard Paris shout.

CHRIS'S PIECES

SHADOW FOLLOWED CHRIS into the barn. "I really should be by the computer in case Jordan calls. He should have told Billy by now. I need to be available if he calls."

Chris turned to face him. Seeing the worry and anxiety in Shadow's face, he delicately said, "That was two days ago. If he hasn't called by now, he's not going to. That should make you happy. It means everything went well."

"I know, but—" Shadow began.

Chris cut him off, knowing the real reason for Shadow's worry. "If you want to contact him, it's okay. Do it. I'm sure Jordan misses you, too."

"What if Billy picks up, or he's there?" Shadow asked, looking away from Chris.

Chris turned Shadow's face, so they were eye to eye. "You have nothing to feel guilty about. Had you not tricked him into leaving and had you not left, you both would probably be dead, too."

"Maybe I could have saved them, maybe taken Mario or Brett with me," Shadow argued weakly. "I could have gone back to see them." Shadow wiped a tear away on his cheek. "Fuck, I've cried more in the last week than I have my entire life."

Chris wiped away a tear on Shadow's other cheek. "Billy didn't go back either. Your lives took you away from the Country Boyz. His took him to Jordan. Yours to me. You have nothing to feel guilty for."

"How did you get to be so poetic?" Shadow asked, sniffling.

Chris answered with a smirk. "I'm an artist. We're sensitive."

"That you are." Shadow leaned in and kissed him. "I love all your sensitive spots."

Chris playfully pushed him away. "Down boy. I still have something to show you."

"Fine," Shadow relented. "Lead the way."

Taking Shadow's hand, Chris led him to the cloth-covered table. "It's a special set. There are two of each piece. One set for us. The other set for, well, I'll let you guess when you see it."

"You never make duplicate pieces," Shadow commented.

Shadow reached for the sheet, but Chris pushed his hand away. "I have to show you them in order or they won't make sense."

"Then get on with it. I'm getting sawdust all over me," Shadow grumbled. Chris lifted the corner of the sheet, revealing two identical pieces. Shadow gasped. He reached out and ran a hand over the intricate woodwork. "Is that?"

Pride filled Chris's voice. "You and Jordan. You on one side of the screen, him on the other." Chris revealed two more pieces. "You and me making the video for Billy, and Billy and Jordan watching us." Chris revealed the last two pieces. "This last one is something I hope will happen soon. Me and Jordan watching on as you and Billy reunite in a big hug."

"They are beautiful." Shadow ran a finger over the carving of him and Billy. "The other set is for…" Shadow looked at Chris.

Chris smiled warmly. "For Billy and Jordan. One day, we'll be able to give it to them."

"One day," Shadow said wistfully. "Thank you for this."

Chris hugged him. "You're welcome."

"Okay, I'm going to start crying again." Shadow laughed, returning the hug. "Enough mushy stuff. We need to get the house ready for the guests we have coming." Shadow pulled back. "They had the oddest request. They don't want us to do any of the cooking. They want to do it."

Mysteriously, Chris said, "Maybe one of them is a chef."

"I'm going to make room for these pieces." Shadow studied Chris for a moment. "What are you up to?"

Innocently, Chris said, "Nothing at all."

27

HAPPILY EVER AFTER

"**THERE ARE FRESH** linens on the bed and towels in the bathroom…" Shadow paused at the bottom of the stairs when he saw Chris looking out the window. "What are you doing?"

Chris turned around and said, "Nothing," failing to sound innocent.

"You're a bad liar." Shadow started toward Chris.

Chris looked back out the window at the sound of a car approaching. "Good! They're here."

"Chris, what's going on?" Shadow was almost to him when Chris turned around, took him by the shoulders, and started guiding him back. "Chris, you're starting to scare me."

Spinning them around so Shadow's back was to the door, Chris nervously said, "Don't be mad at me."

"Okay, you're really freaking me out. What's going on?" Shadow asked insistently.

Chris swallowed hard. "Our guests aren't really guests. I mean, they're guests, but not bed-and-breakfast guests."

"You're not making any sense. They booked on the website." Shadow looked at his husband, baffled.

Chris saw the shadows of the couple coming up the porch. The front door opened. "They're here."

"Hey, Jessie." Shadow's eyes grew wide at the sound of the voice.

Shadow turned around. His heart pounded with excitement. He couldn't believe his eyes. "Paris?" He rushed over and picked up the pint-sized young man. "Paris! Oh! My God! Paris! Why didn't you guys tell me you were coming?!"

"It would have ruined the surprise." Paris hugged him back.

Setting Paris down, Shadow joked, "I would say you're all grown up, but you're still the same size you were when you were thirteen."

"Funny." Paris pushed his glasses back up his nose. "Jessie, Chris. This is my boyfriend, Daniel."

The strikingly handsome young man standing with the luggage waved a hand. "Hello."

"We have so much to catch up on. What have you been up to? How did you pull this off?" Shadow rambled.

Paris pointed over to Chris. "I got Chris's number from your parents and we set this surprise up." He looked over at Chris. Chris gave him a nod. "As for what I've been up to."

"He's been saving a wedding and seducing me," Daniel added cheekily.

Paris glared back at him, then back at Shadow. "He seduced me, but yes, I was saving a wedding." Paris took a deep breath for courage. "If you didn't know, I chose to work in the entertainment field. I actually landed a job with a studio." Paris swallowed hard. "An adult film studio."

"Hey, it's honest work, right?" Shadow said a little nervously. "If you love the work, why not? Right?"

Daniel put a hand on Paris's shoulder. "I, uh, should go get the luggage."

"Isn't that your luggage right there?" Shadow asked, looking at the bags on the floor.

Cryptically, Daniel answered, "Some more baggage just arrived."

"Jessie, I know Billy and Jordan," Paris said slowly. Shadow's face went white. "I was there when Jordan told Billy about your interview."

Shadow shook his head. "No. I can explain."

"You don't owe anyone an explanation." Paris grabbed Shadow's trembling hands. "Billy understood after seeing the videos." Paris smiled warmly. "The next morning, Jordan proposed to Billy. They're engaged."

Shadow felt his heart explode with joy. "That's fantastic news! I am so happy for them!"

"I know you are." Paris glanced back at the sound of the door opening. "We have another surprise for you."

"Why couldn't I drive?" Billy pouted in the passenger seat.

Jordan teased, "Because you drive like a maniac, and I'd like to get there in one piece."

"You're my fiancé now. I wouldn't do anything to harm you." Billy took Jordan's free hand. "Besides, Mom and Dad are looking forward to the wedding."

Jordan glanced over at Billy for a moment. "They really do love you. I love you, Snuggles."

"Say it again." Billy bounced excitedly in his seat. "Say it again."

Jordan turned down the road to the bed-and-breakfast. "I love you, Snuggles."

"I love you, too, Teddy Bear!" Billy gushed with excitement. "I love it when you call me Snuggles." Billy grew serious. "Jordan, I made a decision. I want to take your last name when we get married."

Jordan glanced over at Billy. "Are you sure?"

"I love my mother, but I don't think she'll ever love me the way your parents love me," Billy explained. "Your parents have embraced me like I was their son. I'd rather be a Hudson than a Turner. If I can't be their son by blood, then I can be it in name."

Jordan patted Billy on the leg. "When we go back to see them, I want you to tell them. I think they'll appreciate it."

"I will." Billy looked out the window. "I think we're here."

Jordan parked beside another car. "It was nice of Paris to arrange this little getaway for us."

"Is that Daniel on the porch?" Billy asked, peering out the windshield. "What's he doing here?"

Jordan studied the porch, the red potted hanging flowers, and the purple vines dangling down the door. "There's something familiar about this place."

"Come on, let's see what's going on." Billy jumped out of the car.

Jordan followed behind. Daniel met them at the bottom of the stairs. He looked nervously at Jordan. "Hey guys, I hope you don't mind. Paris and I decided to join you this weekend at his cousin's bed-and-breakfast."

"Not at all." Billy squinted his eyes at Daniel. "Unless you plan on offing us in the woods or something."

Daniel smiled. "Only if you talk about my cooking again."

"Can we get inside?" Jordan interrupted. "It was a long trip, and I'd like to take a shower."

Daniel put up a hand to stop them. "Paris arranged a little surprise. We want you two to be prepared for it."

"What's going on?" Billy asked suspiciously. "Is this a sexy bachelor party? Are you going to give Paris another sexy lap dance in front of us?"

Jordan scolded Billy. "You really should have recorded that for me."

"No, come on. They should be ready." Daniel headed back up the stairs. Billy and Jordan followed. He turned the knob as he said, "Consider this your engagement present from us."

Jordan entered after Daniel. He saw Paris holding someone's hands. He saw another man standing behind them. It hit him who it was, who Paris was with. "Paris's cousin is…"

"Shadow!" Billy exclaimed, rushing past Jordan. Paris stepped aside just in time to avoid Billy. "Oh, my God! Shadow!" He picked Shadow up and spun him around the room.

Shadow cried out, "Billy, I can't believe it's you! It's really you!"

Jordan pointed a finger at Paris. "Your cousin is Shadow."

"Yeah, but I know him by his real name, Jessie." Paris beamed.

Jordan shook his head in disbelief. "Paris's cousin is Shadow."

"He was Shadow," Chris said, coming up to Jordan. "He's Jessie now." He stuck out his hand for Jordan. "It's a pleasure to finally meet you in person."

Jordan took the offered hand, then pulled Chris into a hug. "I can't believe this."

"Oh, but you can believe Alex is dating his uncle?" Daniel teased.

Jordan shot Daniel a look. "Technically, he is."

"How long are we going to leave those two like that?" Paris asked, drawing their attention to the two crying men embracing each other.

Jordan smiled. "As long as they need."

BOOK CLUB QUESTIONS

1. Jordan tends to shy away from public displays of affection with Billy. Do you think it's his insecurities about being with Billy or what he fears people will say about him when they see him with Billy?

2. Billy and Jordan have phone sex. Do you think things like phone sex can keep things spicy in a relationship? Have you tried it?

3. Shadow left because Brett loved his dream more than him. Would you let someone make you their second choice?

4. Should Shadow, or Billy for that matter, have survivor's guilt?

5. Jordan lied about being able to contact Shadow after he told Billy about the interview in order to keep his integrity as a journalist and keep the trust people

have in him. Seeing how upset Billy was, would you be able to keep that secret or would you cave?

6. Jordan talks about his insecurities and issues, and he feels they are hurting Billy. Do you think they are? Why or why not?

7. Jordan says he's famous adjacent even though he's a known writer now. Does he have imposter syndrome?

8. When Chris got injured, he cut himself off from Shadow because he didn't want to see the pity in Shadow's eyes when he saw him. Do you think that was selfish of him?

9. Do you think Shadow really enjoyed making adult films or do you think he liked the attention he got?

10. There's a change in Jordan when he acknowledges his faults and issues. Do you think that by owning our faults and issues, we release the control they have over us?

SPECIAL ACKNOWLEGEMENT AND THANK YOU

I WOULD LIKE TO give a special thank you and acknowledgement to Jason Collins. Watching his YouTube channel, Raw and Uncensored With Masculine Jason, gave me the structure I needed to write portions of this book and showed me how to have the interviewer interact with the interviewee and pose questions in a way that gets the interviewee to open up. For this help he didn't know he gave me, I am eternally grateful. Thank you, Jason.

ROBERT (ROBBY) J. Lewis is a writer based out of Charleston, South Carolina. He has brought you not only the Shadow Guardian series but also the Someone series under Robert Lewis. He has written numerous steamy film scripts for Noir Male and Icon Male. More recently, has agreed to start writing for Luxxxe Studios and is currently producing videos as the Luxxxe Studios Insider. You can keep up with Robby Lewis's latest releases, news, and antics via his social media or at www.robert-j-lewis.com.

More books from 4 Horsemen Publications

LGBT Erotica

Dominic N. Ashen
Steel & Thunder
Storms & Sacrifice
Secrets & Spires
Arenas & Monsters
My Three Orc Dads: a Novella
Before the Storm: a Novella
Service Duty: a Novella

I Think I'm a Serial Swiper
Lookin in All the Wrong Places
What Makes Me a Whore?
A Breach in Confidentiality
Back Door Pass
My European Adventure
An Unexpected Affair
Finding True Love
The Dr. Cage Chronicles

Eskay Kabba
Hidden Love
Not So Hidden
Signs of Affection
Deeply Devoted to Him
Honest Love
A Plane and Simple Connection
A Familiar Family Connection

Leo Sparx
Before Alexander
Claiming Alexander
Taming Alexander
Saving Alexander
The Fall of the House of Otter
The Case of Armando

Grayson Ace
How I Got Here
First Year Out of the Closet
You're Only a Top?
You're Only a Bottom?

Robert Lewis
Someone to Love
Someone to Come Home To
Someone to Kiss
Someone to Marry

Discover more at
4HorsemenPublications.com